King Lear

William Shakespeare

SADDLEBACK
EDUCATIONAL PUBLISHING

Saddleback's *Illustrated Classics*™

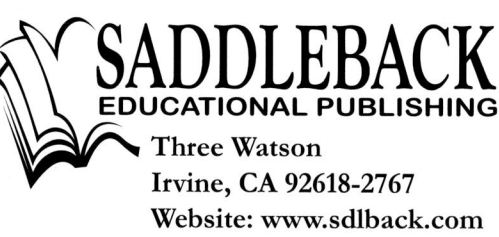

SADDLEBACK
EDUCATIONAL PUBLISHING
Three Watson
Irvine, CA 92618-2767
Website: www.sdlback.com

ISBN: 1-59905-147-8

Printed in China

Welcome to
Saddleback's *Illustrated Classics*™

We are proud to welcome you to Saddleback's *Illustrated Classics*™. Saddleback's *Illustrated Classics*™ was designed specifically for the classroom to introduce readers to many of the great classics in literature. Each text, written and adapted by teachers and researchers, has been edited using the Dale-Chall vocabulary system. In addition, much time and effort has been spent to ensure that these high-interest stories retain all of the excitement, intrigue, and adventure of the original books.

With these graphically *Illustrated Classics*™, you learn what happens in the story in a number of different ways. One way is by reading the words a character says. Another way is by looking at the drawings of the character. The artist can tell you what kind of person a character is and what he or she is thinking or feeling.

This series will help you to develop confidence and a sense of accomplishment as you finish each novel. The stories in Saddleback's *Illustrated Classics*™ are fun to read. And remember, fun motivates!

Overview

Everyone deserves to read the best literature our language has to offer. Saddleback's *Illustrated Classics*™ was designed to acquaint readers with the most famous stories from the world's greatest authors, while teaching essential skills. You will learn how to:

- Establish a purpose for reading
- Activate prior knowledge
- Evaluate your reading
- Listen to the language as it is written
- Extend literary and language appreciation through discussion and writing activities.

Reading is one of the most important skills you will ever learn. It provides the key to all kinds of information. By reading the *Illustrated Classics*™, you will develop confidence and the self-satisfaction that comes from accomplishment—a solid foundation for any reader.

Remember,

"Today's readers are tomorrow's leaders."

William Shakespeare

William Shakespeare was baptized on April 26, 1564, in Stratford-on-Avon, England, the third child of John Shakespeare, a well-to-do merchant, and Mary Arden, his wife. Young William probably attended the Stratford grammar school, where he learned English, Greek, and a great deal of Latin. Historians aren't sure of the exact date of Shakespeare's birth.

In 1582, Shakespeare married Anne Hathaway. By 1583 the couple had a daughter, Susanna, and two years later the twins, Hamnet and Judith. Somewhere between 1585 and 1592 Shakespeare went to London, where he became first an actor and then a playwright. His acting company, *The King's Men*, appeared most often in the *Globe* theater, a part of which Shakespeare himself owned.

In all, Shakespeare is believed to have written thirty-seven plays, several nondramatic poems, and a number of sonnets. In 1611 when he left the active life of the theater, he returned to Stratford and became a country gentleman, living in the second-largest house in town. For five years he lived a quiet life. Then, on April 23, 1616, William Shakespeare died and was buried in Trinity Church in Stratford. From his own time to the present, Shakespeare is considered one of the greatest writers of the English-speaking world.

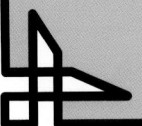
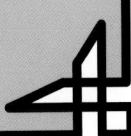

William Shakespeare

King Lear

GONERIL

KING LEAR

KENT

EDGAR

REGAN

EDMUND

CORDELIA

GLOUCESTER

NEARLY TWO THOUSAND YEARS AGO, OLD KING LEAR RULED BRITAIN. HE HAD THREE DAUGHTERS: GONERIL, REGAN, AND CORDELIA.

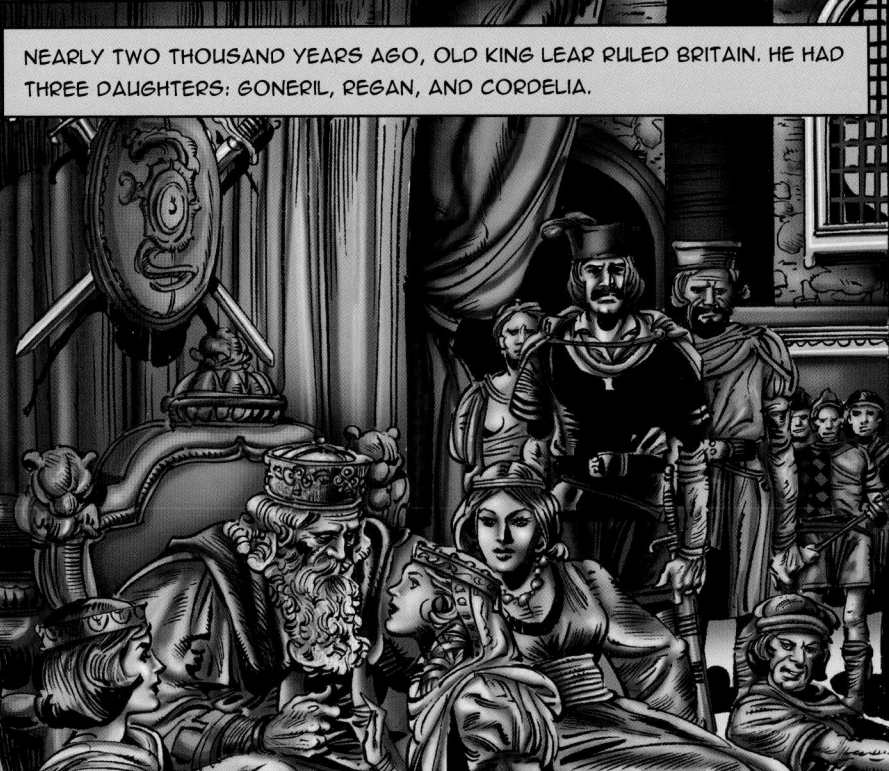

LEAR HAD ALWAYS BEEN A MAN WHO ACTED WITHOUT THINKING THINGS THROUGH. BECAUSE OF THIS, HE WAS ABOUT TO MAKE ONE OF THE BIGGEST MISTAKES OF HIS LIFE.

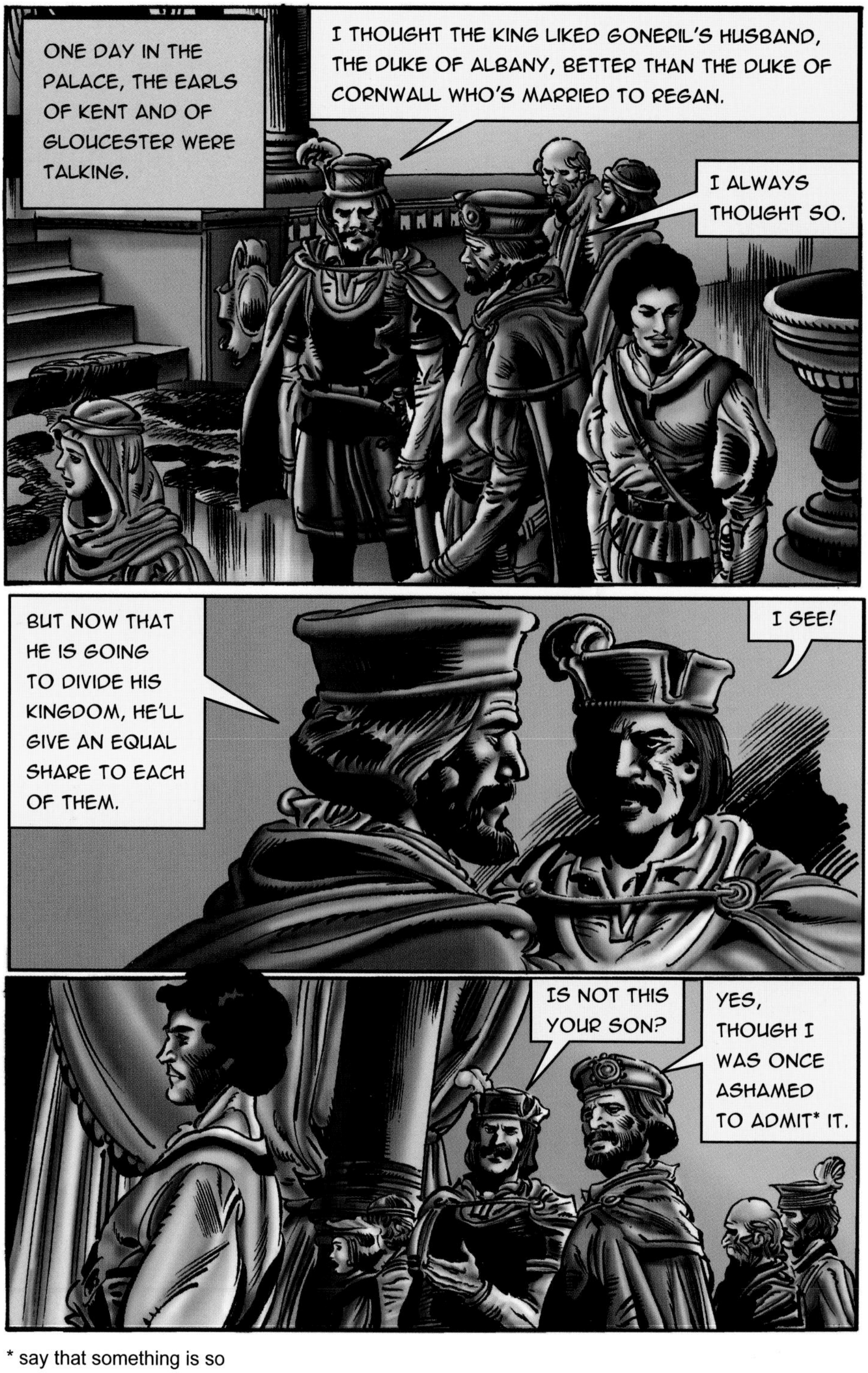
ONE DAY IN THE PALACE, THE EARLS OF KENT AND OF GLOUCESTER WERE TALKING.
I THOUGHT THE KING LIKED GONERIL'S HUSBAND, THE DUKE OF ALBANY, BETTER THAN THE DUKE OF CORNWALL WHO'S MARRIED TO REGAN.
I ALWAYS THOUGHT SO.
BUT NOW THAT HE IS GOING TO DIVIDE HIS KINGDOM, HE'LL GIVE AN EQUAL SHARE TO EACH OF THEM.
I SEE!
IS NOT THIS YOUR SON?
YES, THOUGH I WAS ONCE ASHAMED TO ADMIT* IT.

* say that something is so

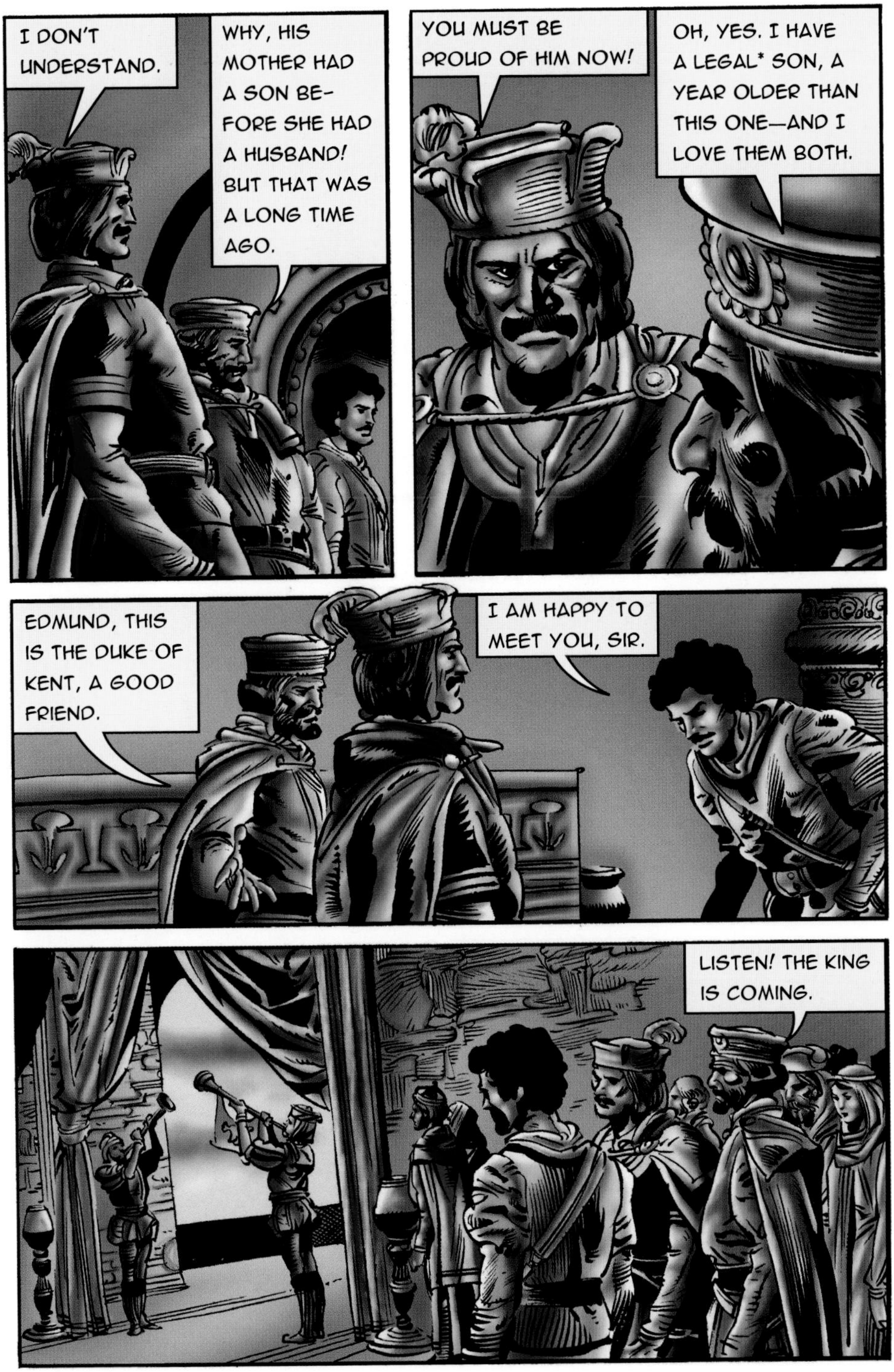
I DON'T UNDERSTAND.
WHY, HIS MOTHER HAD A SON BEFORE SHE HAD A HUSBAND! BUT THAT WAS A LONG TIME AGO.
YOU MUST BE PROUD OF HIM NOW!
OH, YES. I HAVE A LEGAL* SON, A YEAR OLDER THAN THIS ONE—AND I LOVE THEM BOTH.
EDMUND, THIS IS THE DUKE OF KENT, A GOOD FRIEND.
I AM HAPPY TO MEET YOU, SIR.
LISTEN! THE KING IS COMING.

* according to the law

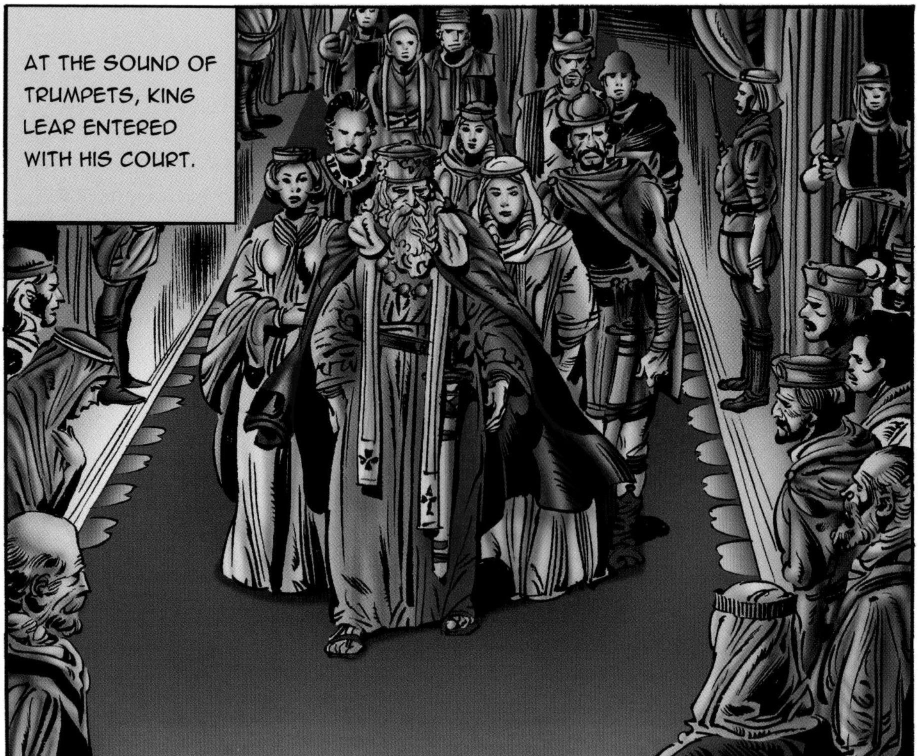
AT THE SOUND OF TRUMPETS, KING LEAR ENTERED WITH HIS COURT.

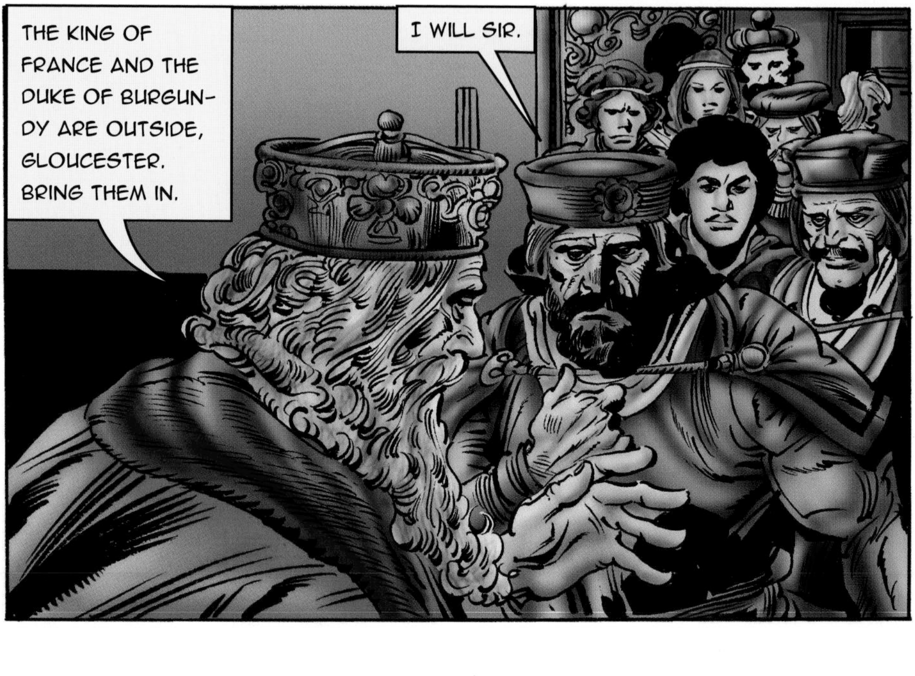
THE KING OF FRANCE AND THE DUKE OF BURGUNDY ARE OUTSIDE, GLOUCESTER. BRING THEM IN.
I WILL SIR.

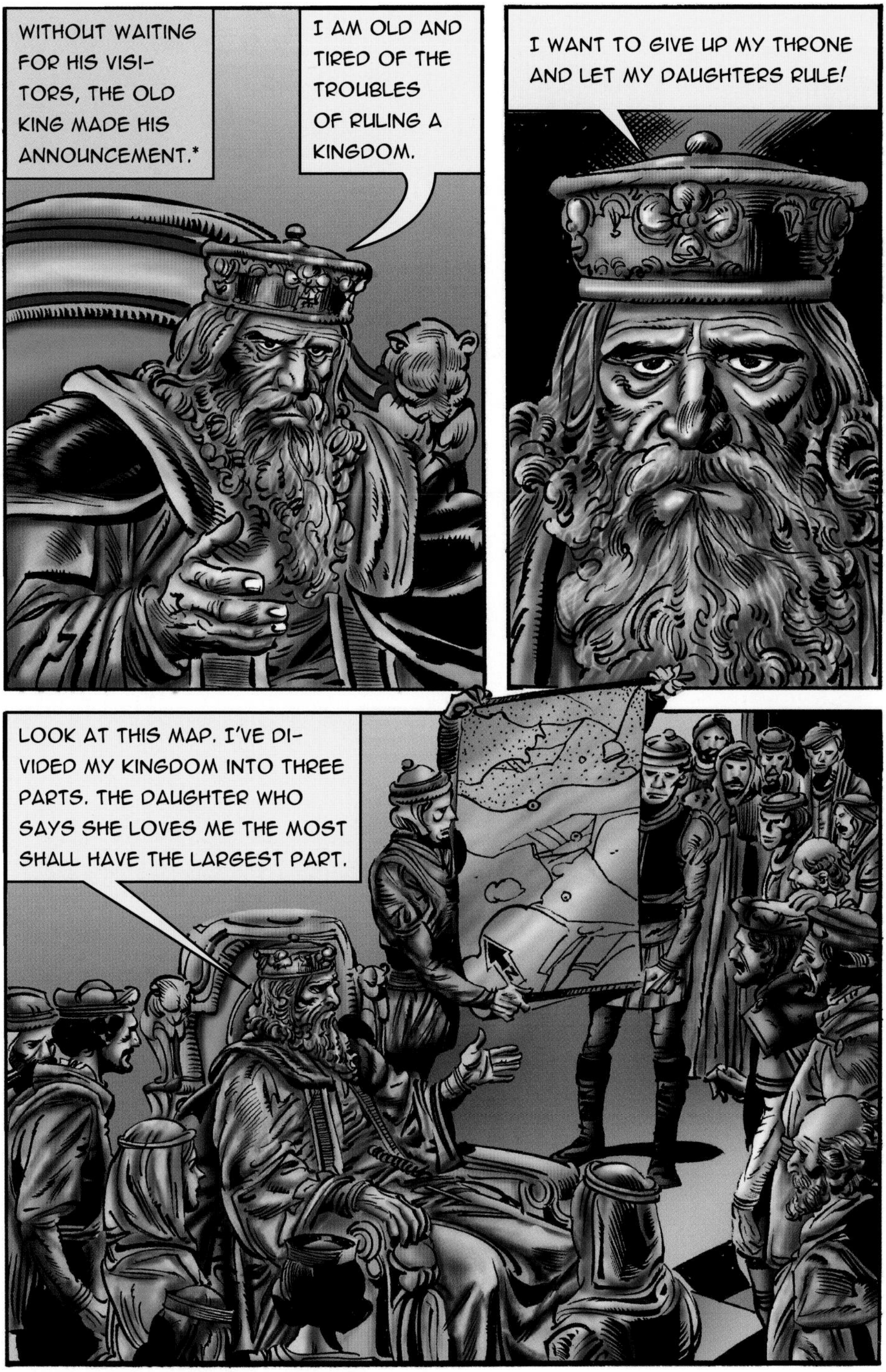
WITHOUT WAITING FOR HIS VISI-TORS, THE OLD KING MADE HIS ANNOUNCEMENT.*
I AM OLD AND TIRED OF THE TROUBLES OF RULING A KINGDOM.
I WANT TO GIVE UP MY THRONE AND LET MY DAUGHTERS RULE!
LOOK AT THIS MAP. I'VE DI-VIDED MY KINGDOM INTO THREE PARTS. THE DAUGHTER WHO SAYS SHE LOVES ME THE MOST SHALL HAVE THE LARGEST PART.

* a statement made before a group of people

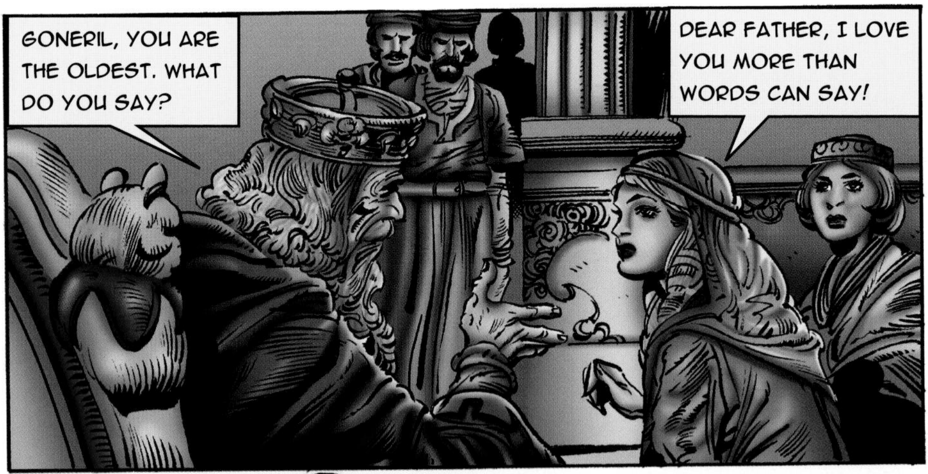
GONERIL, YOU ARE THE OLDEST. WHAT DO YOU SAY?
DEAR FATHER, I LOVE YOU MORE THAN WORDS CAN SAY!

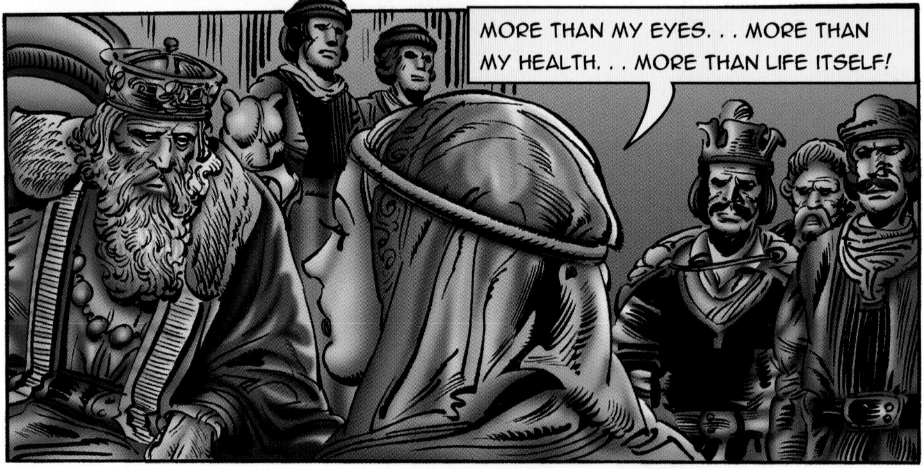
MORE THAN MY EYES. . . MORE THAN MY HEALTH. . . MORE THAN LIFE ITSELF!

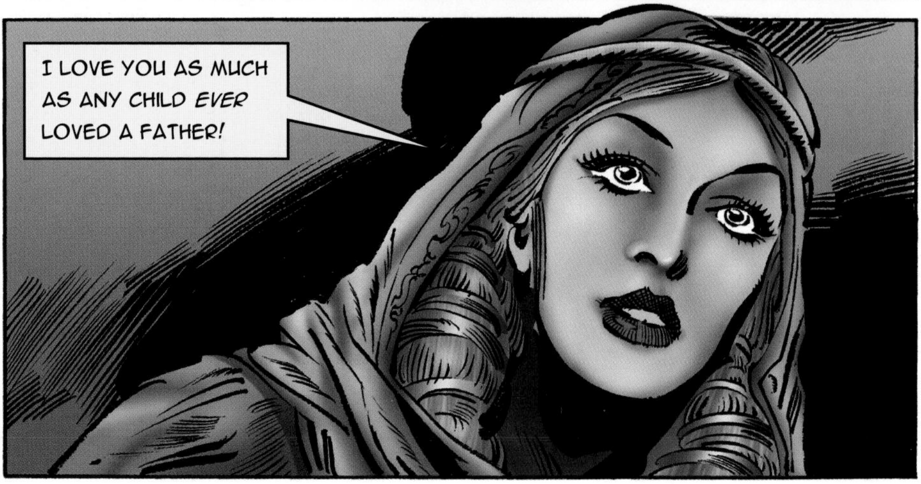
I LOVE YOU AS MUCH AS ANY CHILD *EVER* LOVED A FATHER!

I AM PLEASED! I WILL GIVE YOU AND YOUR CHILDREN ALL THE RICH LAND BETWEEN THESE LINES ON THE MAP.

THANK YOU, DEAR FATHER.

THEN KING LEAR TURNED TO HIS SECOND DAUGHTER.

NOW OUR DEAREST REGAN, WIFE OF THE DUKE OF CORNWALL. . . WHAT DO *YOU* SAY?

I FEEL AS MY SISTER DOES.

SHE DESCRIBES* MY LOVE FOR YOU EXACTLY—BUT SHE SAYS TOO LITTLE.

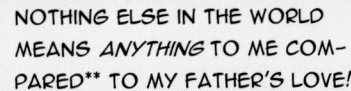

NOTHING ELSE IN THE WORLD MEANS *ANYTHING* TO ME COMPARED** TO MY FATHER'S LOVE!

* explains, shows, tells about
** showing how two things are alike or different

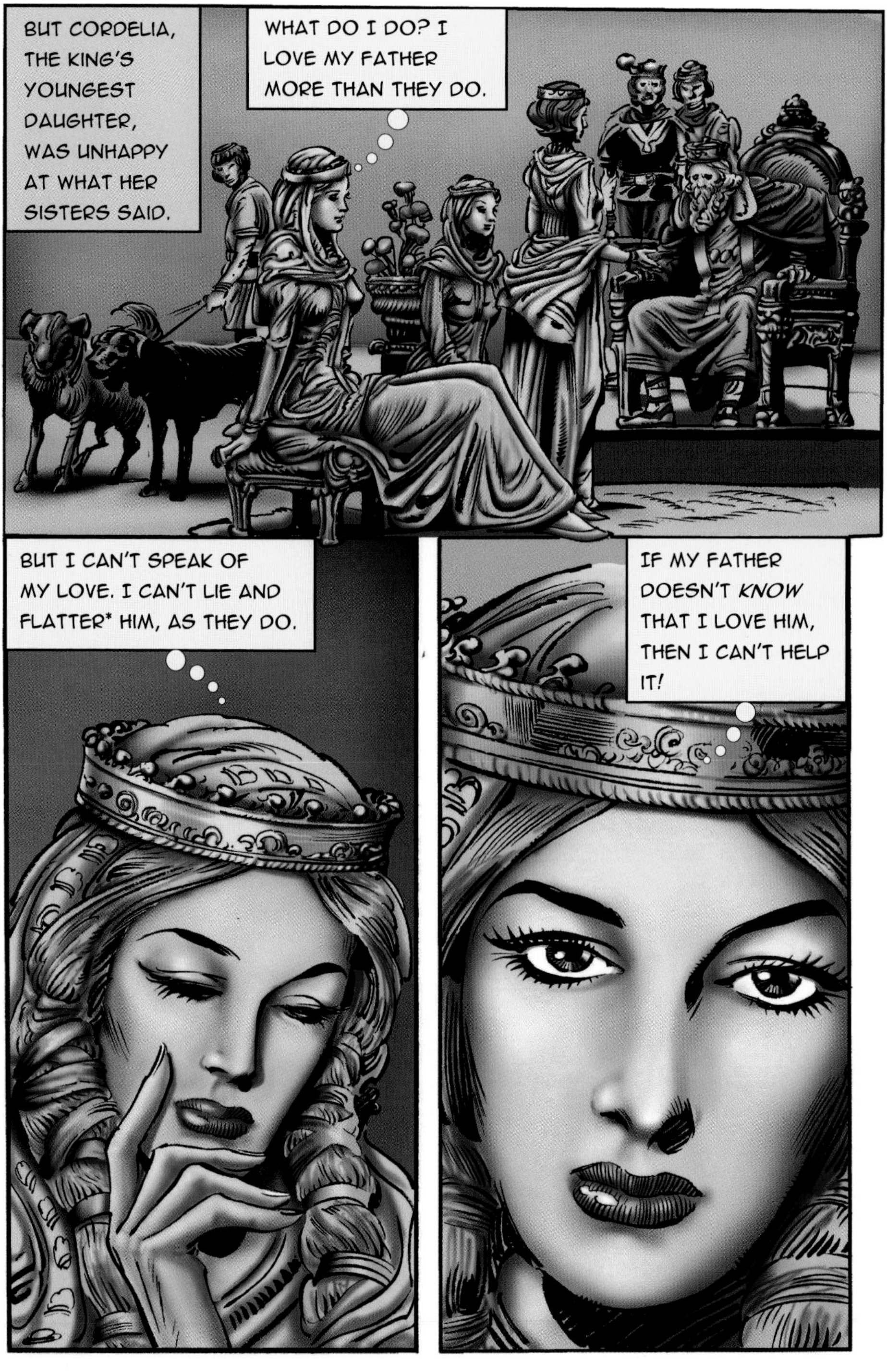
BUT CORDELIA, THE KING'S YOUNGEST DAUGHTER, WAS UNHAPPY AT WHAT HER SISTERS SAID.
WHAT DO I DO? I LOVE MY FATHER MORE THAN THEY DO.
BUT I CAN'T SPEAK OF MY LOVE. I CAN'T LIE AND FLATTER* HIM, AS THEY DO.
IF MY FATHER DOESN'T *KNOW* THAT I LOVE HIM, THEN I CAN'T HELP IT!

* make someone think he is better than he really is

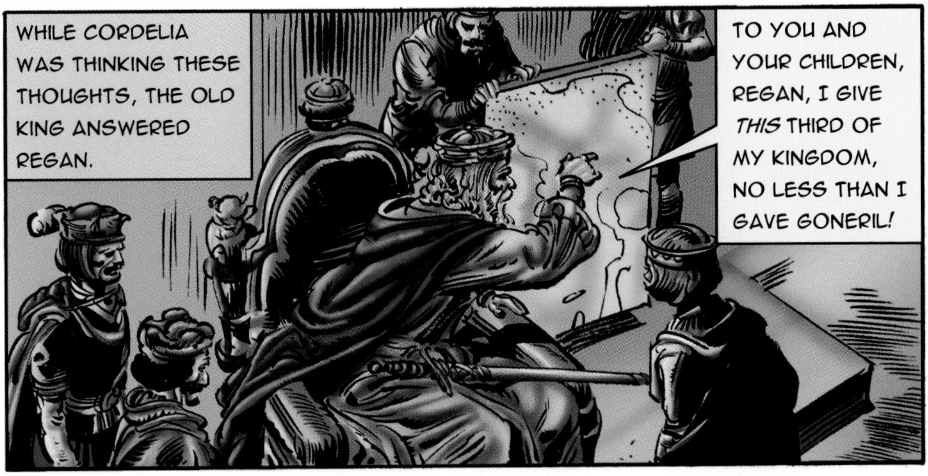
WHILE CORDELIA WAS THINKING THESE THOUGHTS, THE OLD KING ANSWERED REGAN.
TO YOU AND YOUR CHILDREN, REGAN, I GIVE *THIS* THIRD OF MY KINGDOM, NO LESS THAN I GAVE GONERIL!

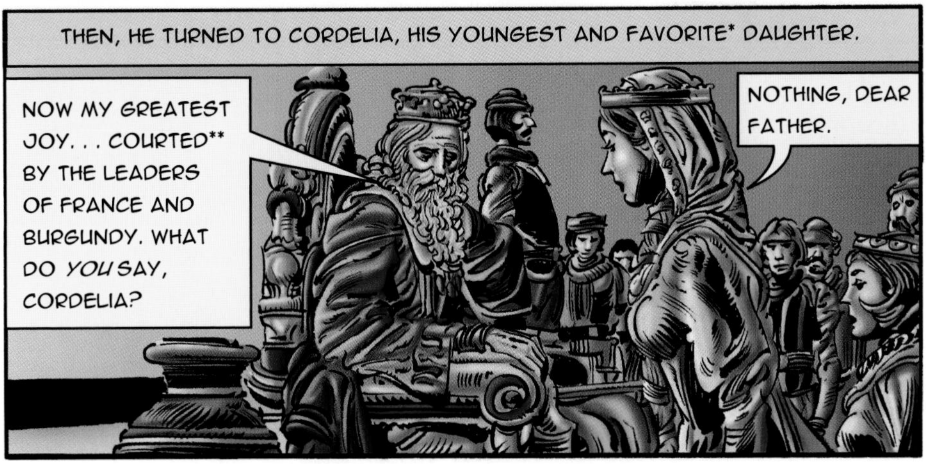
THEN, HE TURNED TO CORDELIA, HIS YOUNGEST AND FAVORITE* DAUGHTER.
NOW MY GREATEST JOY. . . COURTED** BY THE LEADERS OF FRANCE AND BURGUNDY. WHAT DO *YOU* SAY, CORDELIA?
NOTHING, DEAR FATHER.

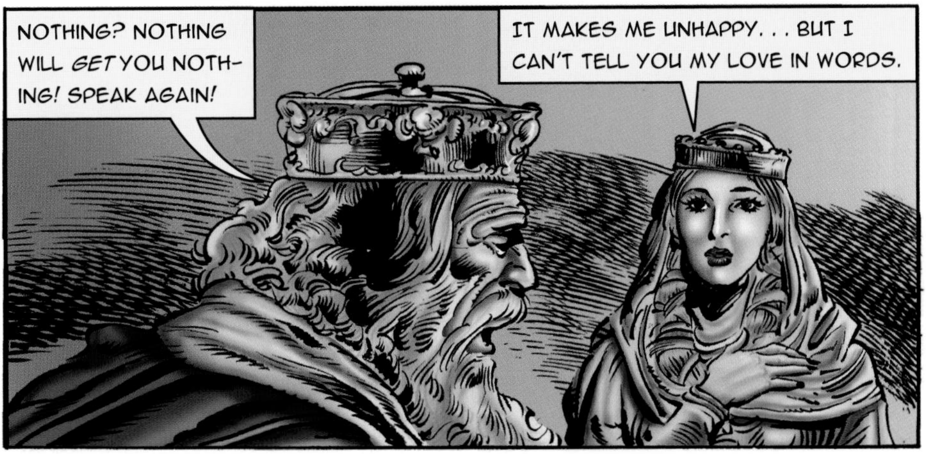
NOTHING? NOTHING WILL *GET* YOU NOTH-ING! SPEAK AGAIN!
IT MAKES ME UNHAPPY. . . BUT I CAN'T TELL YOU MY LOVE IN WORDS.

* best loved

** sought after in marriage

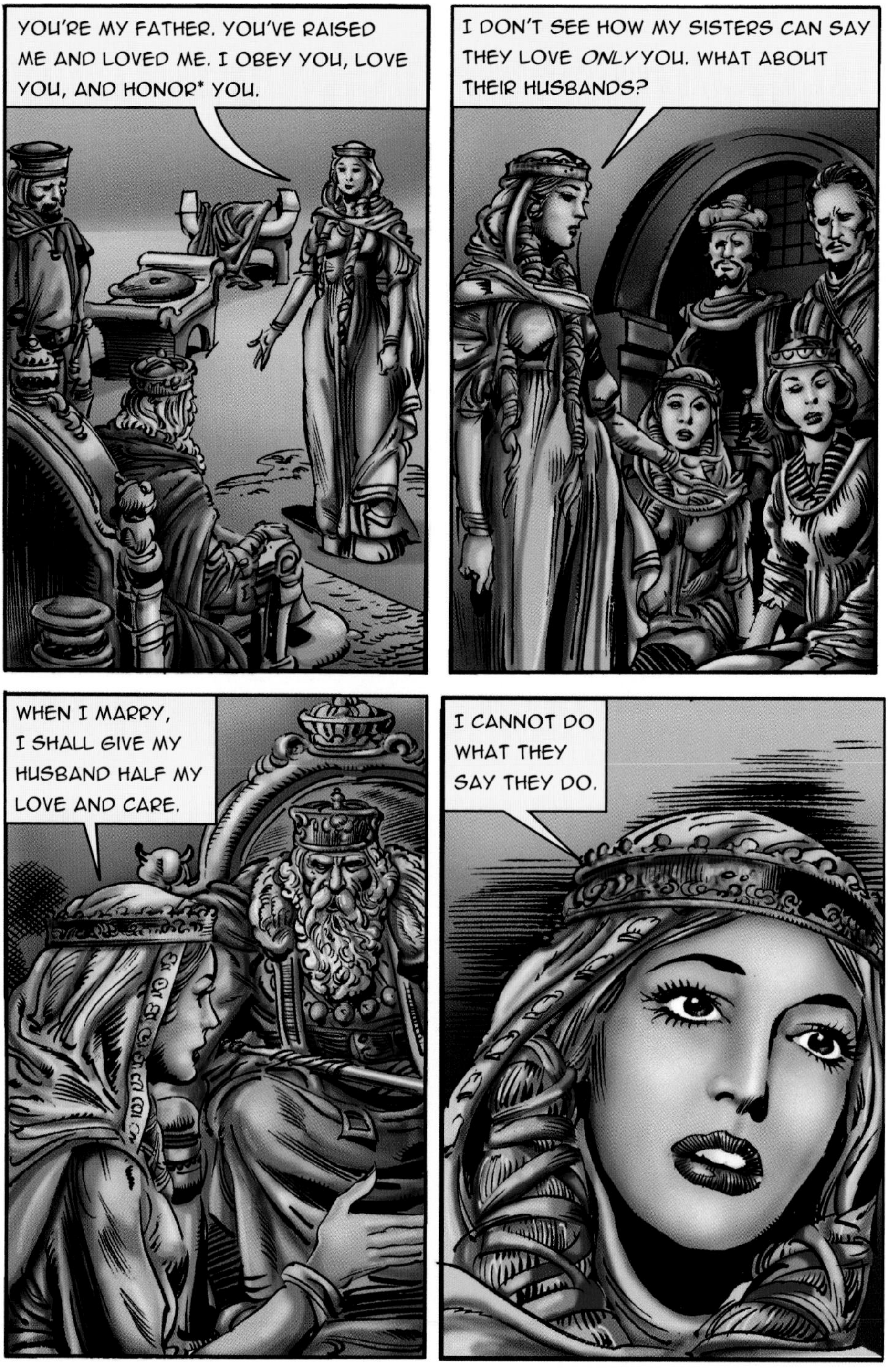
YOU'RE MY FATHER. YOU'VE RAISED ME AND LOVED ME. I OBEY YOU, LOVE YOU, AND HONOR* YOU.
I DON'T SEE HOW MY SISTERS CAN SAY THEY LOVE *ONLY* YOU. WHAT ABOUT THEIR HUSBANDS?
WHEN I MARRY, I SHALL GIVE MY HUSBAND HALF MY LOVE AND CARE.
I CANNOT DO WHAT THEY SAY THEY DO.

* respect

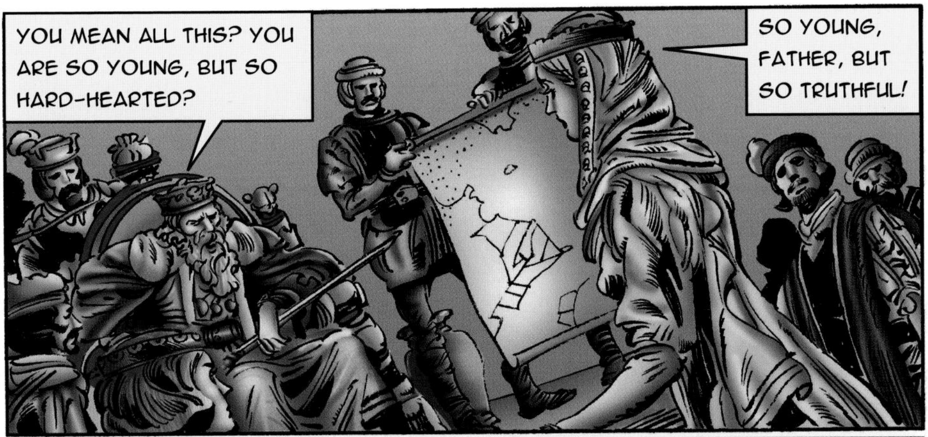
YOU MEAN ALL THIS? YOU ARE SO YOUNG, BUT SO HARD-HEARTED?
SO YOUNG, FATHER, BUT SO TRUTHFUL!

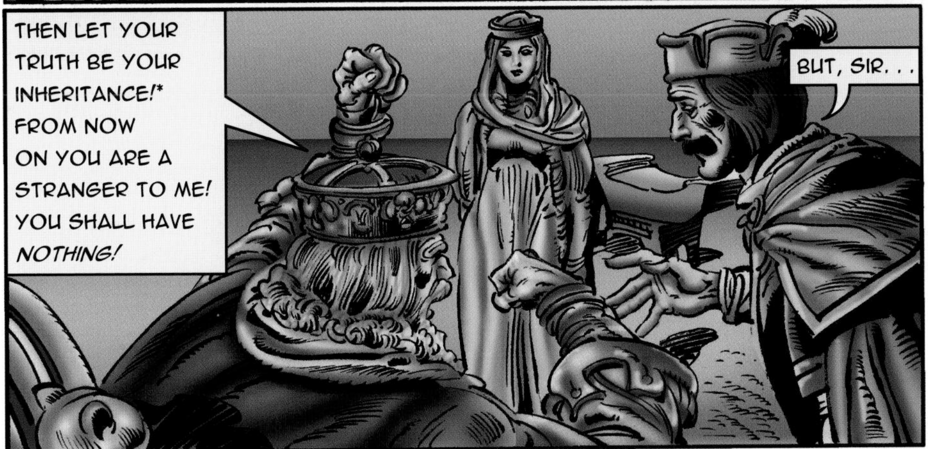
THEN LET YOUR TRUTH BE YOUR INHERITANCE!* FROM NOW ON YOU ARE A STRANGER TO ME! YOU SHALL HAVE *NOTHING!*
BUT, SIR. . .

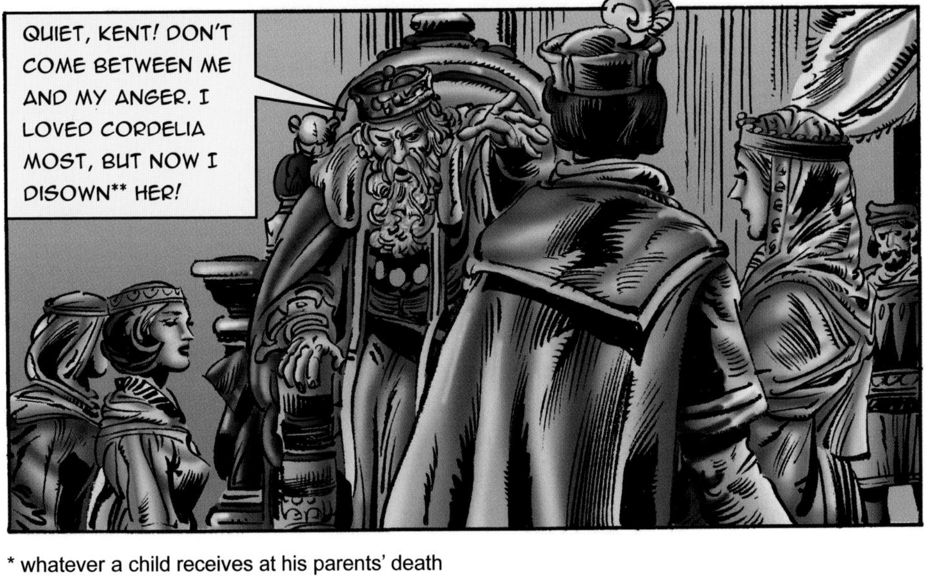
QUIET, KENT! DON'T COME BETWEEN ME AND MY ANGER. I LOVED CORDELIA MOST, BUT NOW I DISOWN** HER!

* whatever a child receives at his parents' death

** have nothing more to do with

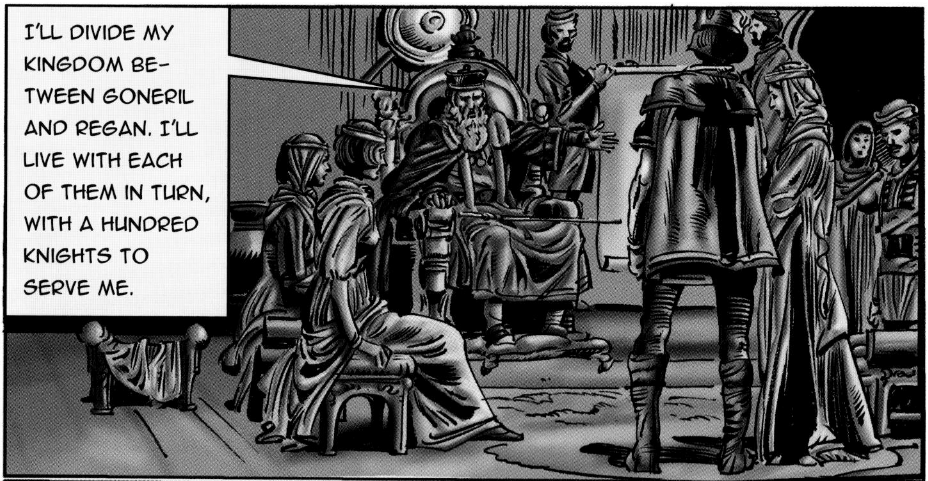
I'LL DIVIDE MY KINGDOM BE- TWEEN GONERIL AND REGAN. I'LL LIVE WITH EACH OF THEM IN TURN, WITH A HUNDRED KNIGHTS TO SERVE ME.

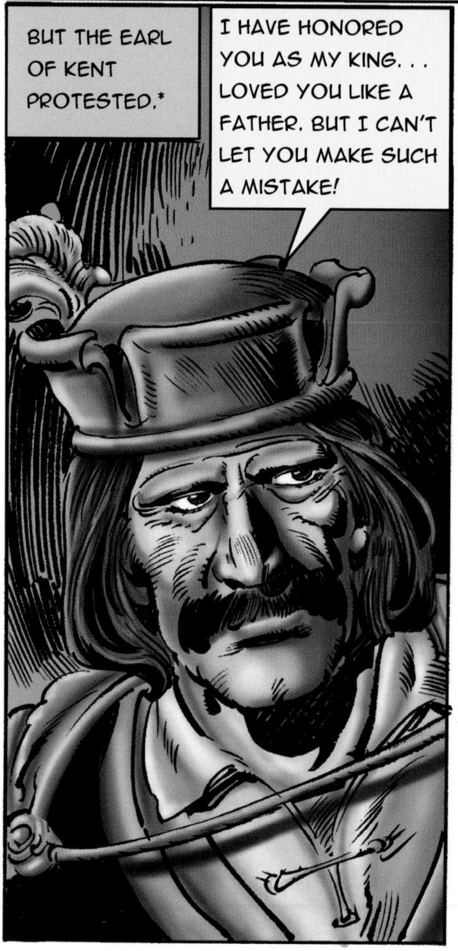
BUT THE EARL OF KENT PROTESTED.*
I HAVE HONORED YOU AS MY KING. . . LOVED YOU LIKE A FATHER. BUT I CAN'T LET YOU MAKE SUCH A MISTAKE!

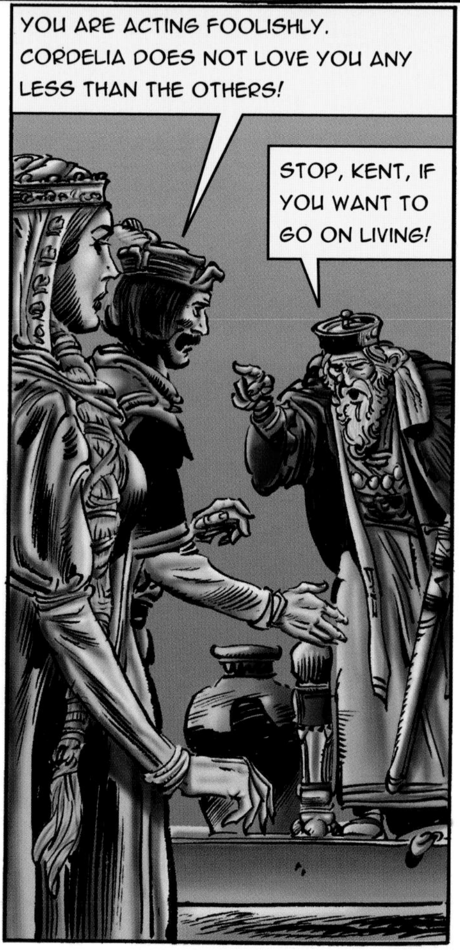
YOU ARE ACTING FOOLISHLY. CORDELIA DOES NOT LOVE YOU ANY LESS THAN THE OTHERS!
STOP, KENT, IF YOU WANT TO GO ON LIVING!

* objected, did not agree

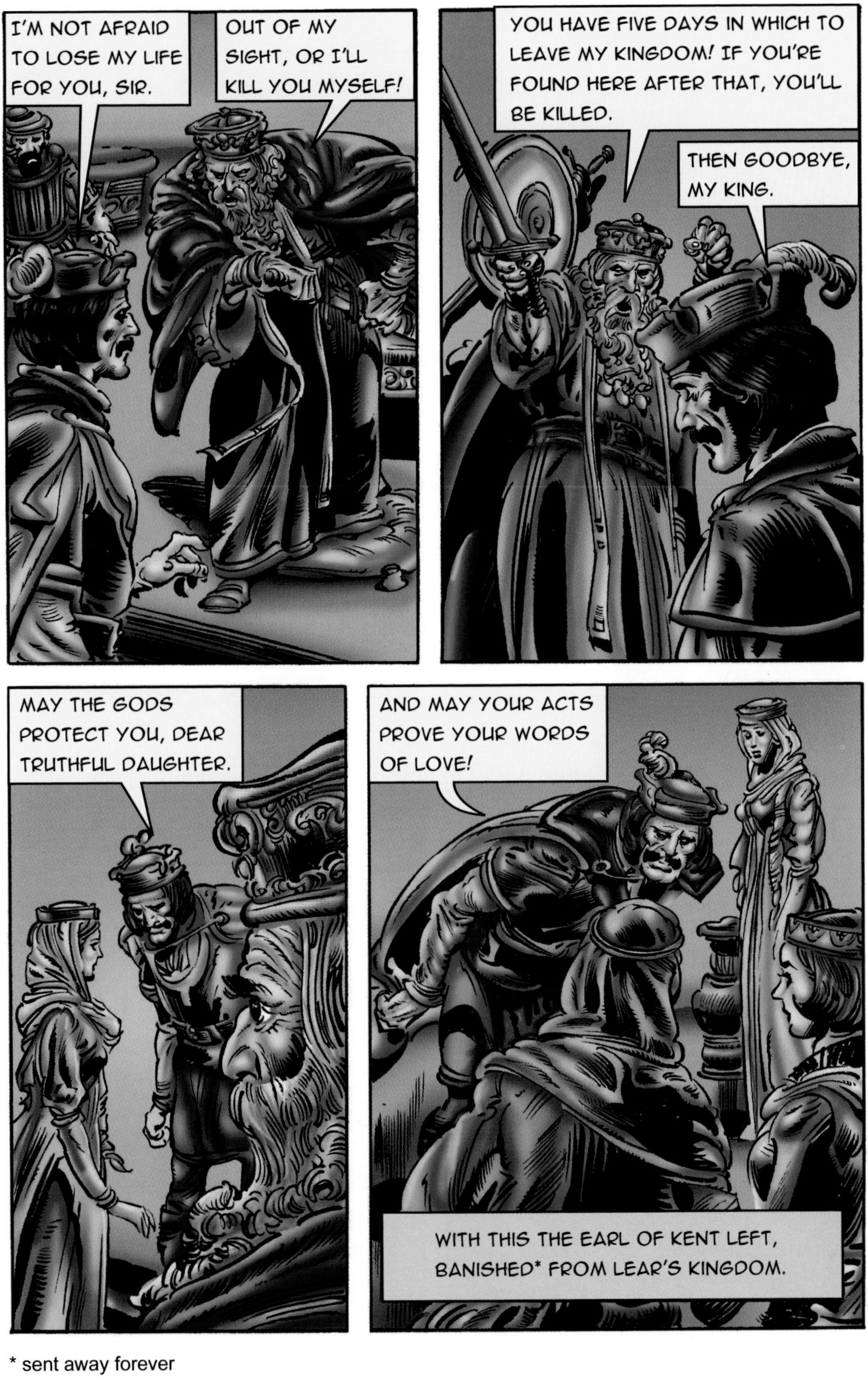
I'M NOT AFRAID TO LOSE MY LIFE FOR YOU, SIR.
OUT OF MY SIGHT, OR I'LL KILL YOU MYSELF!
YOU HAVE FIVE DAYS IN WHICH TO LEAVE MY KINGDOM! IF YOU'RE FOUND HERE AFTER THAT, YOU'LL BE KILLED.
THEN GOODBYE, MY KING.
MAY THE GODS PROTECT YOU, DEAR TRUTHFUL DAUGHTER.
AND MAY YOUR ACTS PROVE YOUR WORDS OF LOVE!
WITH THIS THE EARL OF KENT LEFT, BANISHED* FROM LEAR'S KINGDOM.

* sent away forever

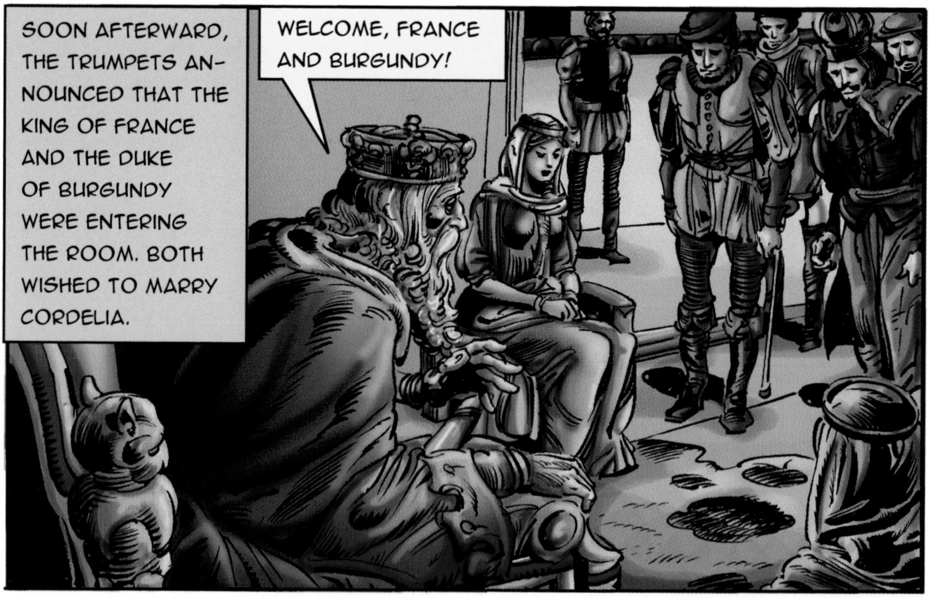
SOON AFTERWARD, THE TRUMPETS ANNOUNCED THAT THE KING OF FRANCE AND THE DUKE OF BURGUNDY WERE ENTERING THE ROOM. BOTH WISHED TO MARRY CORDELIA.
WELCOME, FRANCE AND BURGUNDY!

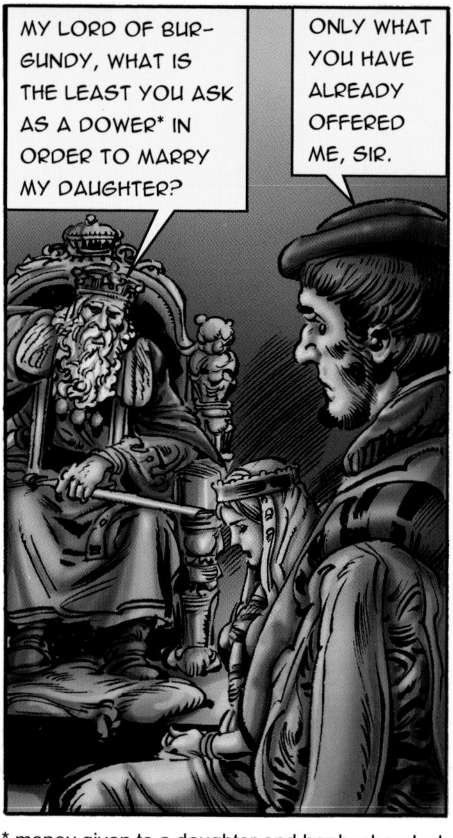
MY LORD OF BURGUNDY, WHAT IS THE LEAST YOU ASK AS A DOWER* IN ORDER TO MARRY MY DAUGHTER?
ONLY WHAT YOU HAVE ALREADY OFFERED ME, SIR.

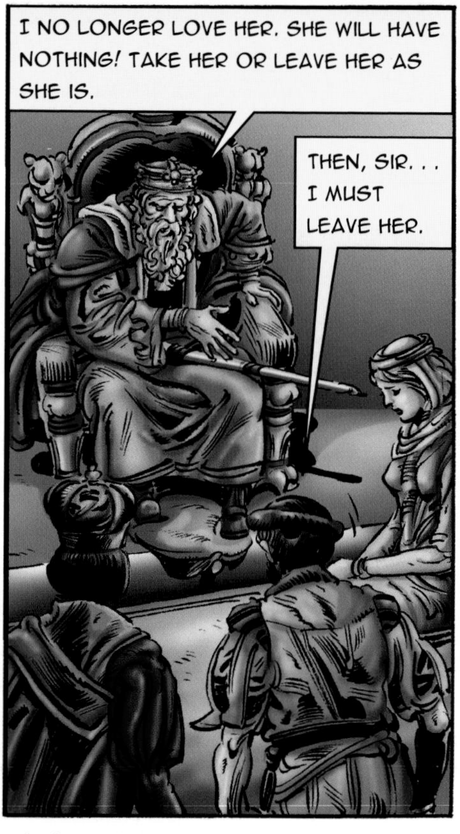
I NO LONGER LOVE HER. SHE WILL HAVE NOTHING! TAKE HER OR LEAVE HER AS SHE IS.
THEN, SIR. . . I MUST LEAVE HER.

* money given to a daughter and her husband when she is married

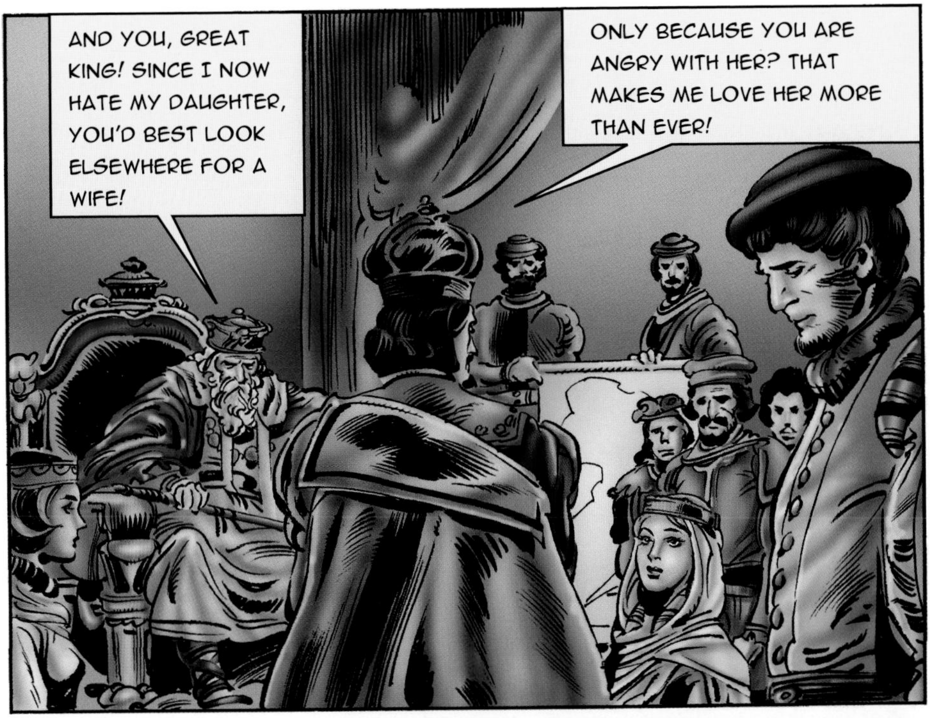
AND YOU, GREAT KING! SINCE I NOW HATE MY DAUGHTER, YOU'D BEST LOOK ELSEWHERE FOR A WIFE!
ONLY BECAUSE YOU ARE ANGRY WITH HER? THAT MAKES ME LOVE HER MORE THAN EVER!

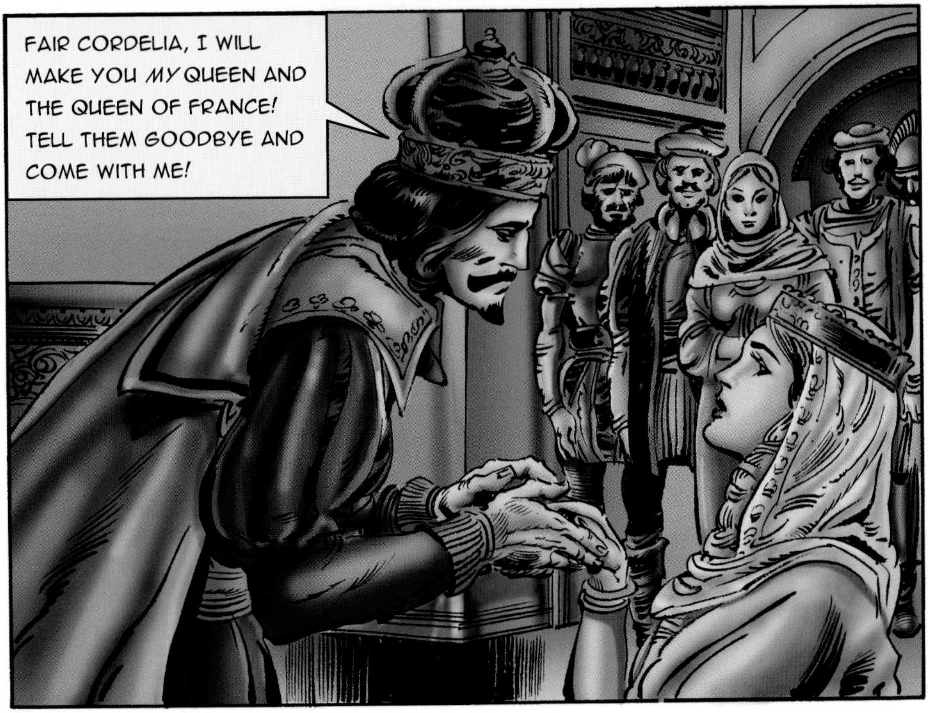
FAIR CORDELIA, I WILL MAKE YOU *MY* QUEEN AND THE QUEEN OF FRANCE! TELL THEM GOODBYE AND COME WITH ME!

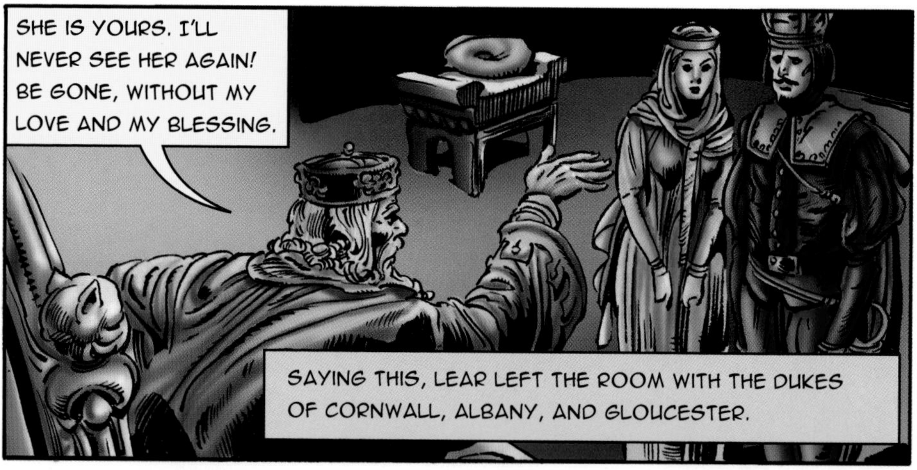
SHE IS YOURS. I'LL NEVER SEE HER AGAIN! BE GONE, WITHOUT MY LOVE AND MY BLESSING.
SAYING THIS, LEAR LEFT THE ROOM WITH THE DUKES OF CORNWALL, ALBANY, AND GLOUCESTER.

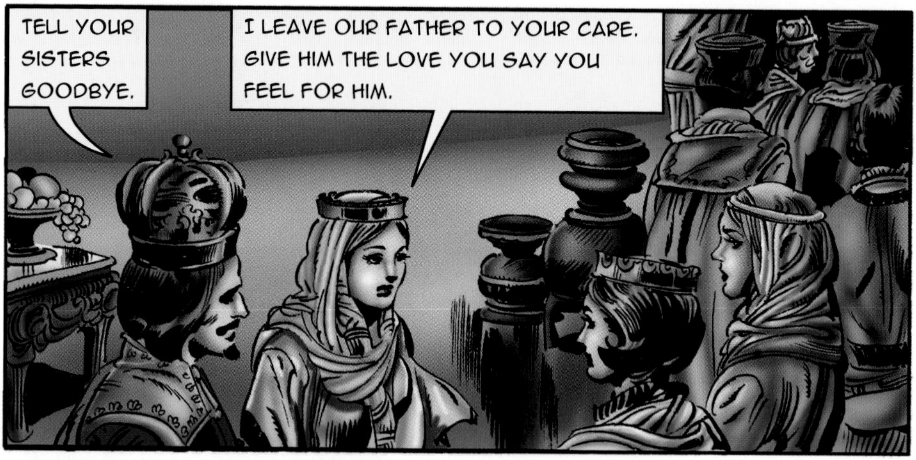
TELL YOUR SISTERS GOODBYE.
I LEAVE OUR FATHER TO YOUR CARE. GIVE HIM THE LOVE YOU SAY YOU FEEL FOR HIM.

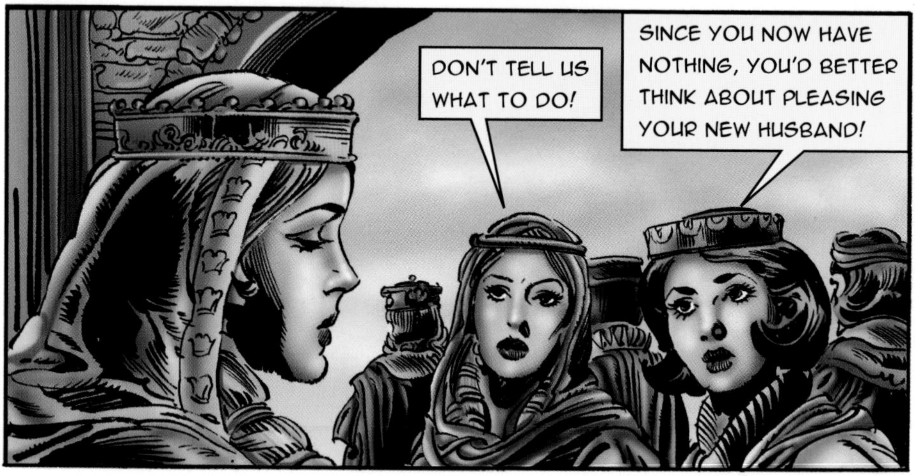
DON'T TELL US WHAT TO DO!
SINCE YOU NOW HAVE NOTHING, YOU'D BETTER THINK ABOUT PLEASING YOUR NEW HUSBAND!

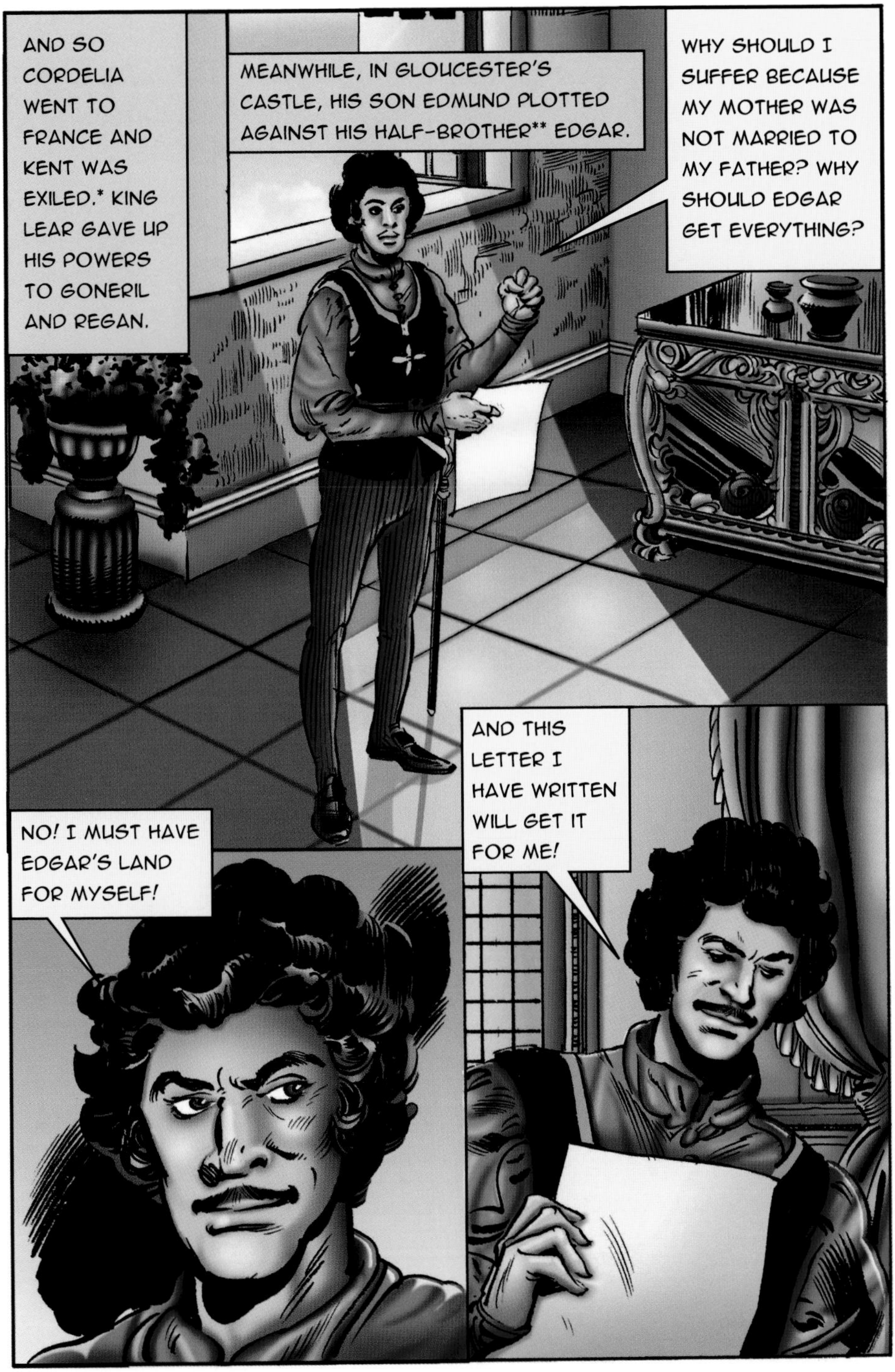
AND SO CORDELIA WENT TO FRANCE AND KENT WAS EXILED.* KING LEAR GAVE UP HIS POWERS TO GONERIL AND REGAN.
MEANWHILE, IN GLOUCESTER'S CASTLE, HIS SON EDMUND PLOTTED AGAINST HIS HALF-BROTHER** EDGAR.
WHY SHOULD I SUFFER BECAUSE MY MOTHER WAS NOT MARRIED TO MY FATHER? WHY SHOULD EDGAR GET EVERYTHING?
NO! I MUST HAVE EDGAR'S LAND FOR MYSELF!
AND THIS LETTER I HAVE WRITTEN WILL GET IT FOR ME!

* sent away

** a brother who shares only one parent with another brother or sister

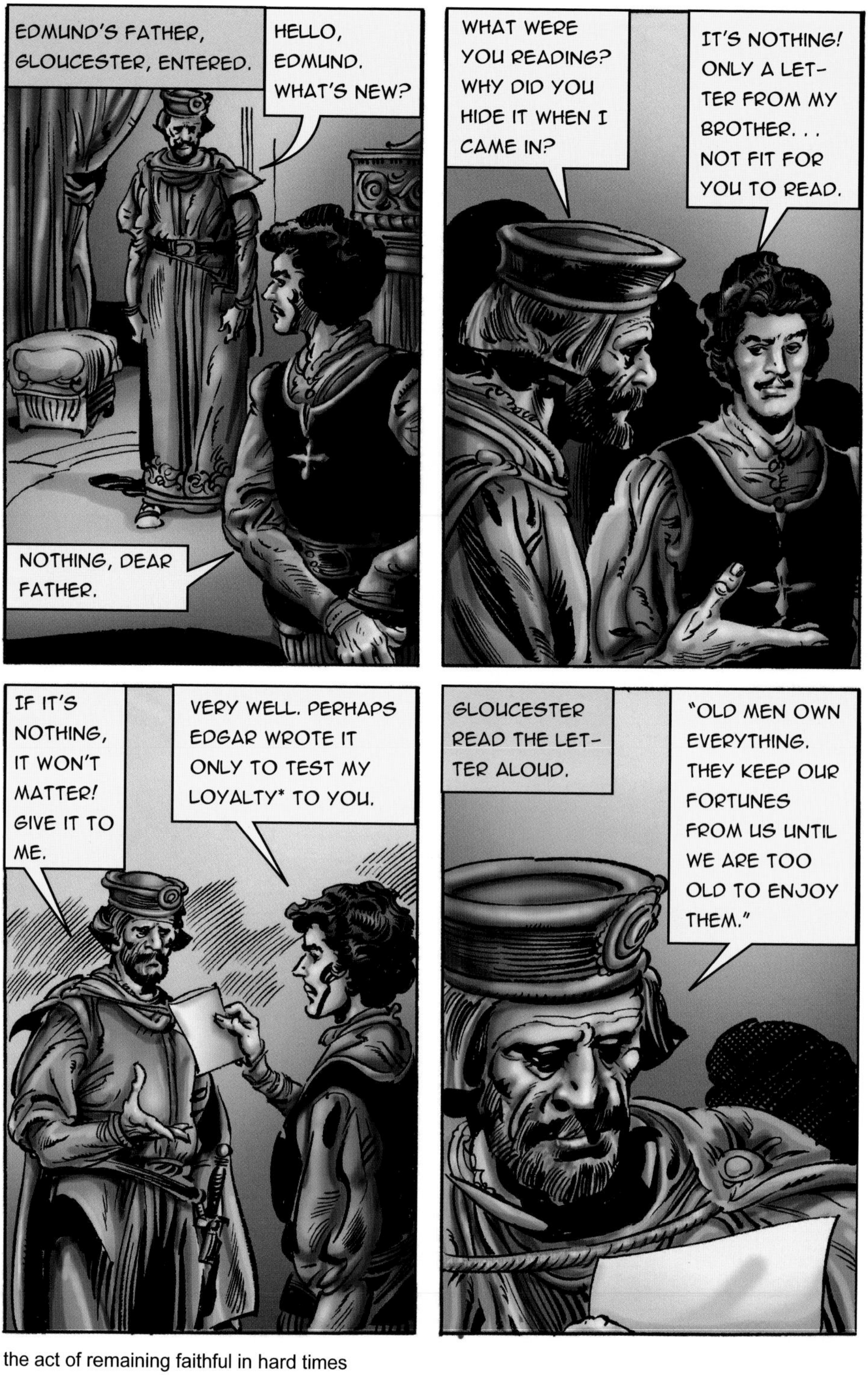
EDMUND'S FATHER, GLOUCESTER, ENTERED.
HELLO, EDMUND. WHAT'S NEW?
NOTHING, DEAR FATHER.
WHAT WERE YOU READING? WHY DID YOU HIDE IT WHEN I CAME IN?
IT'S NOTHING! ONLY A LET-TER FROM MY BROTHER. . . NOT FIT FOR YOU TO READ.
IF IT'S NOTHING, IT WON'T MATTER! GIVE IT TO ME.
VERY WELL. PERHAPS EDGAR WROTE IT ONLY TO TEST MY LOYALTY* TO YOU.
GLOUCESTER READ THE LET-TER ALOUD.
"OLD MEN OWN EVERYTHING. THEY KEEP OUR FORTUNES FROM US UNTIL WE ARE TOO OLD TO ENJOY THEM."

* the act of remaining faithful in hard times

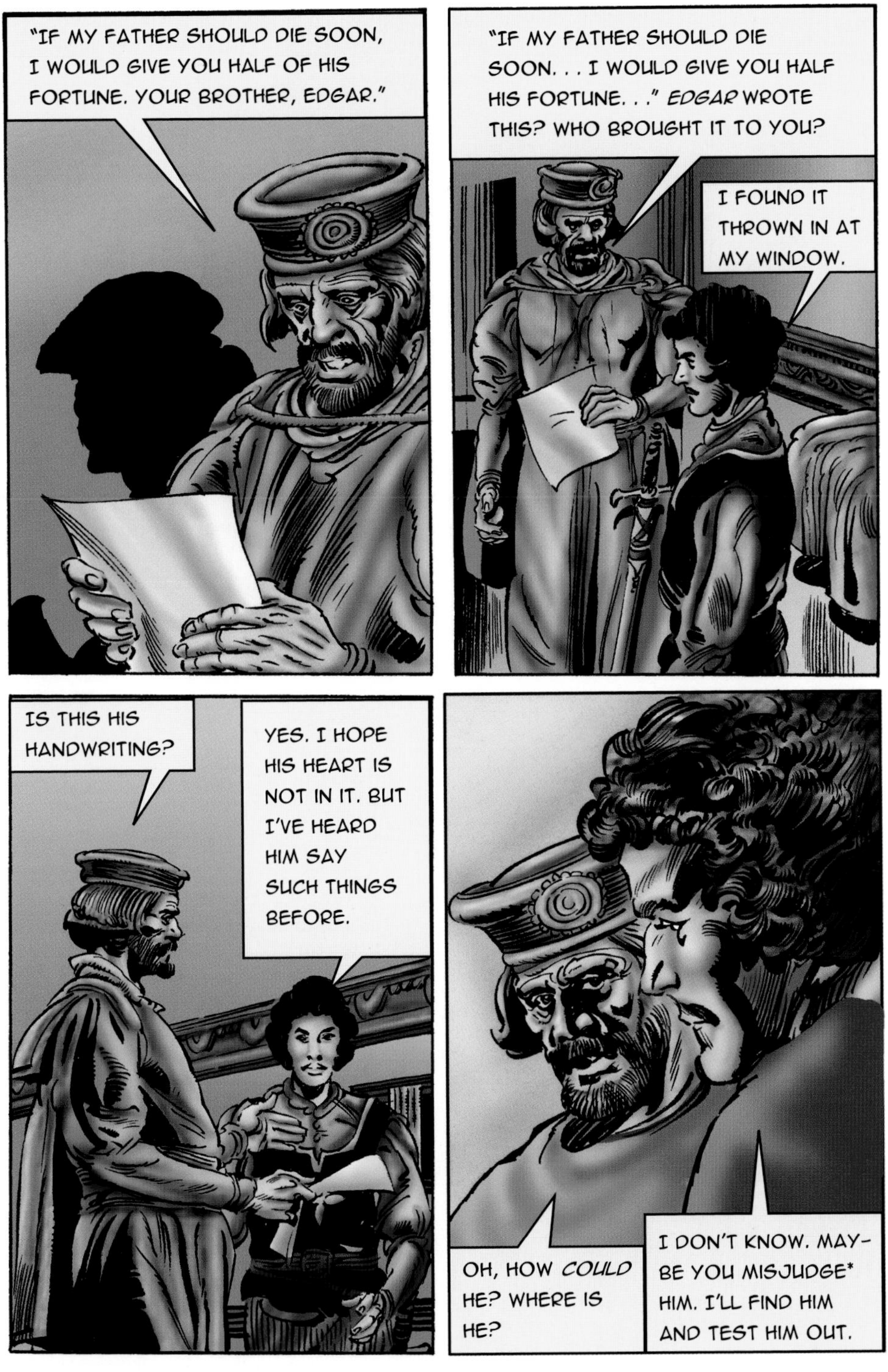
"IF MY FATHER SHOULD DIE SOON, I WOULD GIVE YOU HALF OF HIS FORTUNE. YOUR BROTHER, EDGAR."
"IF MY FATHER SHOULD DIE SOON. . . I WOULD GIVE YOU HALF HIS FORTUNE. . ." *EDGAR* WROTE THIS? WHO BROUGHT IT TO YOU?
I FOUND IT THROWN IN AT MY WINDOW.
IS THIS HIS HANDWRITING?
YES. I HOPE HIS HEART IS NOT IN IT. BUT I'VE HEARD HIM SAY SUCH THINGS BEFORE.
OH, HOW *COULD* HE? WHERE IS HE?
I DON'T KNOW. MAY-BE YOU MISJUDGE* HIM. I'LL FIND HIM AND TEST HIM OUT.

* believe someone to be different from what he really is

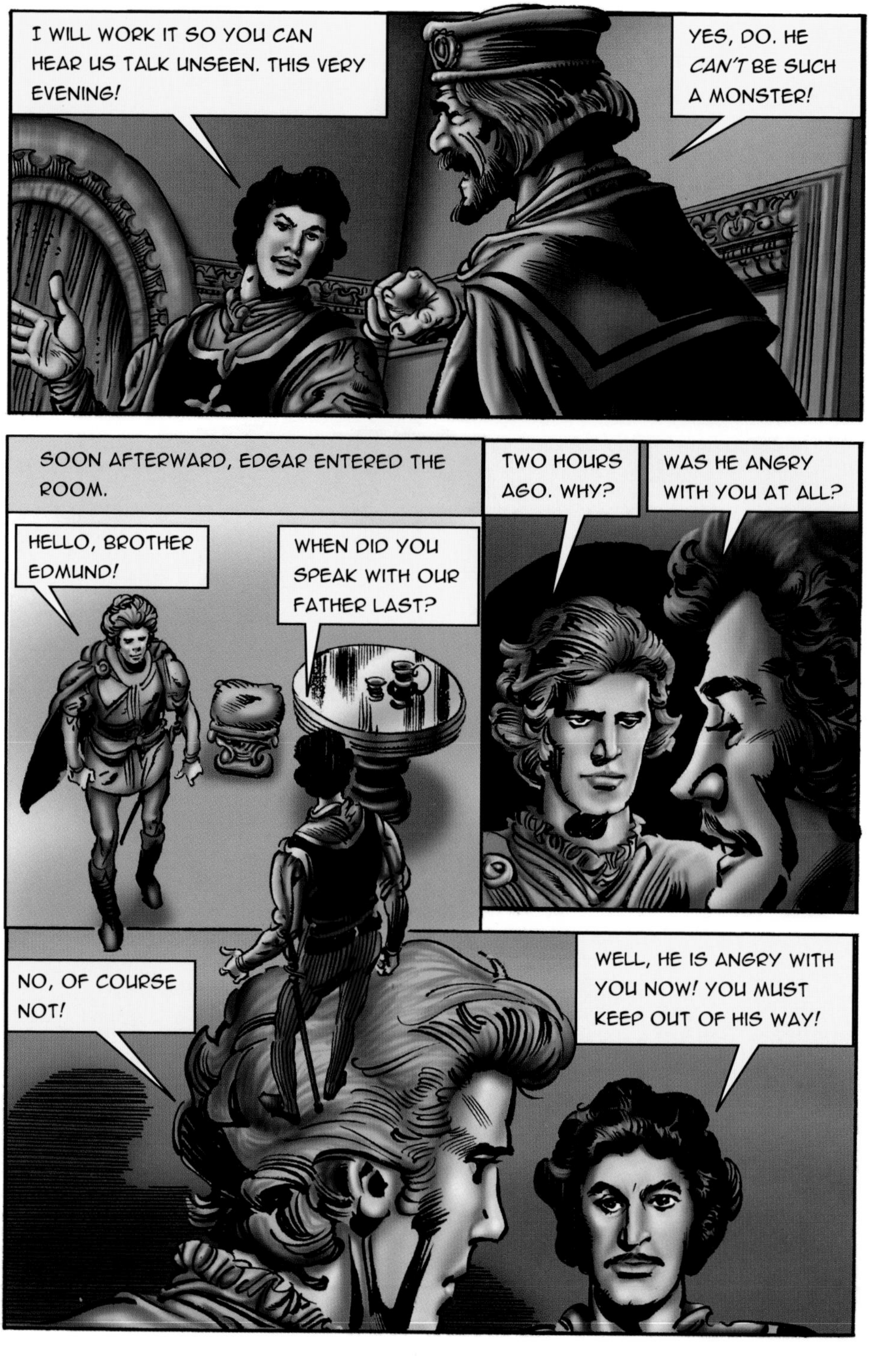
I WILL WORK IT SO YOU CAN HEAR US TALK UNSEEN. THIS VERY EVENING!
YES, DO. HE *CAN'T* BE SUCH A MONSTER!
SOON AFTERWARD, EDGAR ENTERED THE ROOM.
HELLO, BROTHER EDMUND!
WHEN DID YOU SPEAK WITH OUR FATHER LAST?
TWO HOURS AGO. WHY?
WAS HE ANGRY WITH YOU AT ALL?
NO, OF COURSE NOT!
WELL, HE IS ANGRY WITH YOU NOW! YOU MUST KEEP OUT OF HIS WAY!

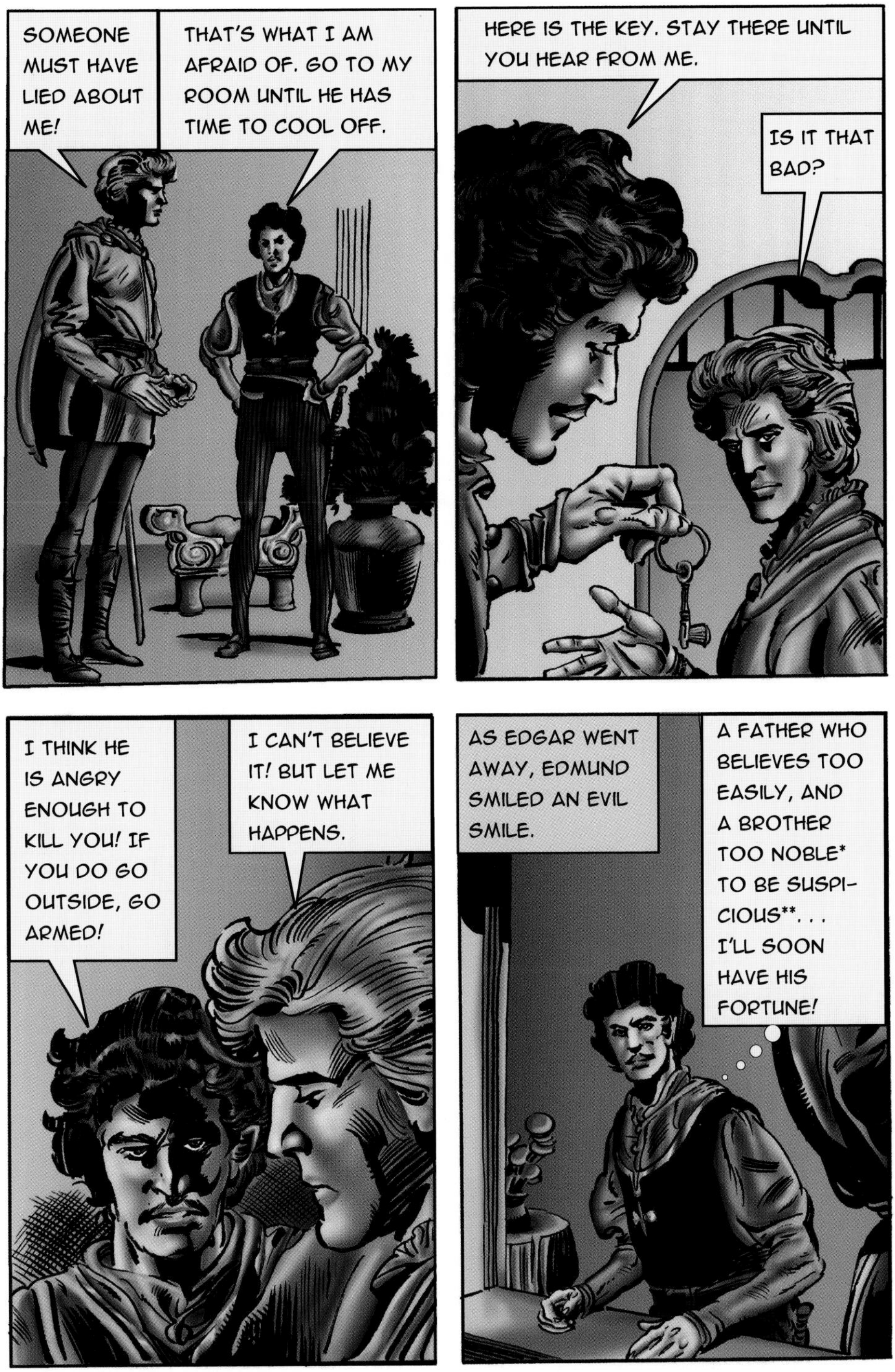
SOMEONE MUST HAVE LIED ABOUT ME!
THAT'S WHAT I AM AFRAID OF. GO TO MY ROOM UNTIL HE HAS TIME TO COOL OFF.
HERE IS THE KEY. STAY THERE UNTIL YOU HEAR FROM ME.
IS IT THAT BAD?
I THINK HE IS ANGRY ENOUGH TO KILL YOU! IF YOU DO GO OUTSIDE, GO ARMED!
I CAN'T BELIEVE IT! BUT LET ME KNOW WHAT HAPPENS.
AS EDGAR WENT AWAY, EDMUND SMILED AN EVIL SMILE.
A FATHER WHO BELIEVES TOO EASILY, AND A BROTHER TOO NOBLE* TO BE SUSPICIOUS**. . . I'LL SOON HAVE HIS FORTUNE!

* good and honest

** thinking evil of someone

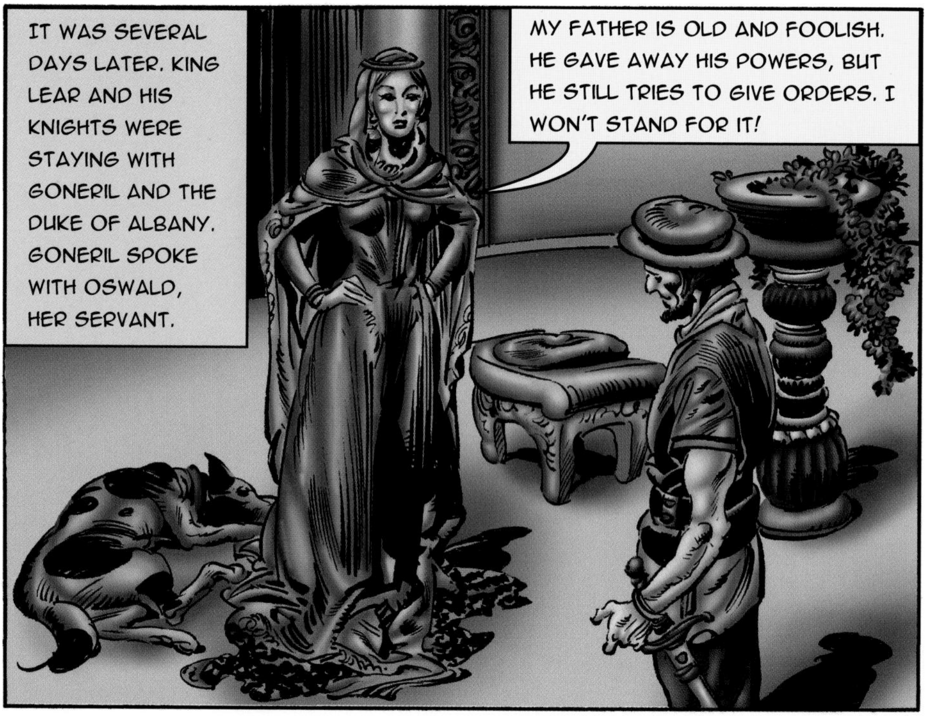
IT WAS SEVERAL DAYS LATER. KING LEAR AND HIS KNIGHTS WERE STAYING WITH GONERIL AND THE DUKE OF ALBANY. GONERIL SPOKE WITH OSWALD, HER SERVANT.
MY FATHER IS OLD AND FOOLISH. HE GAVE AWAY HIS POWERS, BUT HE STILL TRIES TO GIVE ORDERS. I WON'T STAND FOR IT!

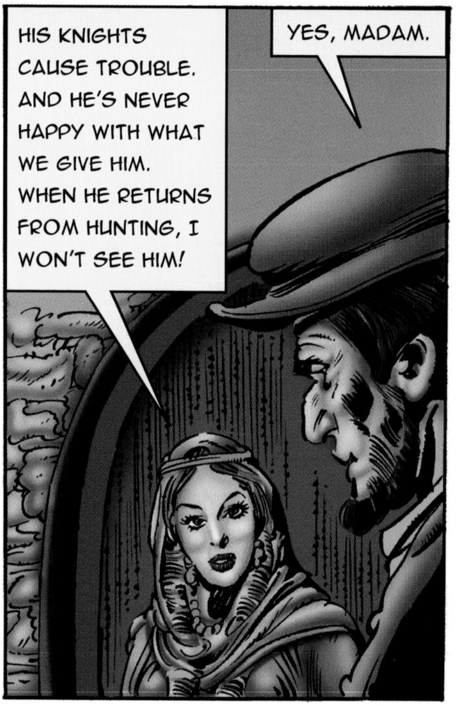
HIS KNIGHTS CAUSE TROUBLE. AND HE'S NEVER HAPPY WITH WHAT WE GIVE HIM. WHEN HE RETURNS FROM HUNTING, I WON'T SEE HIM!
YES, MADAM.

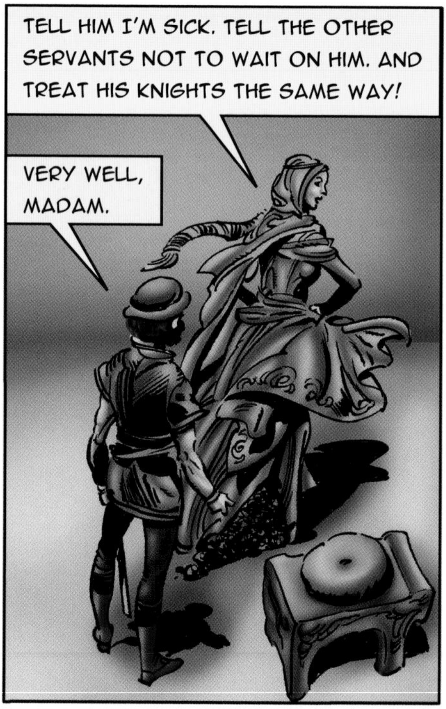
TELL HIM I'M SICK. TELL THE OTHER SERVANTS NOT TO WAIT ON HIM. AND TREAT HIS KNIGHTS THE SAME WAY!
VERY WELL, MADAM.

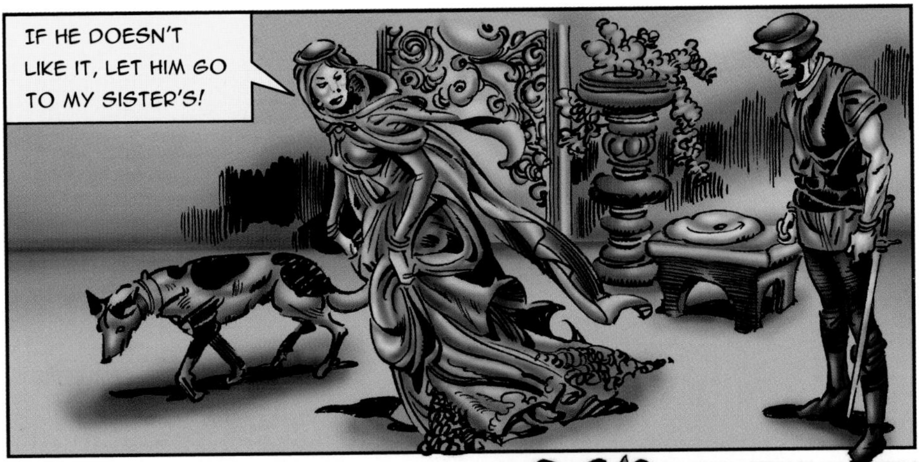
IF HE DOESN'T LIKE IT, LET HIM GO TO MY SISTER'S!

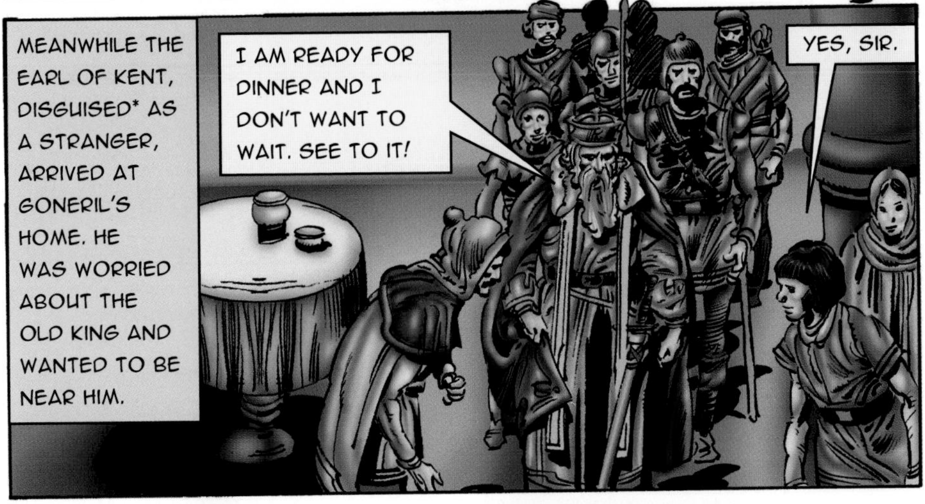
MEANWHILE THE EARL OF KENT, DISGUISED* AS A STRANGER, ARRIVED AT GONERIL'S HOME. HE WAS WORRIED ABOUT THE OLD KING AND WANTED TO BE NEAR HIM.
I AM READY FOR DINNER AND I DON'T WANT TO WAIT. SEE TO IT!
YES, SIR.

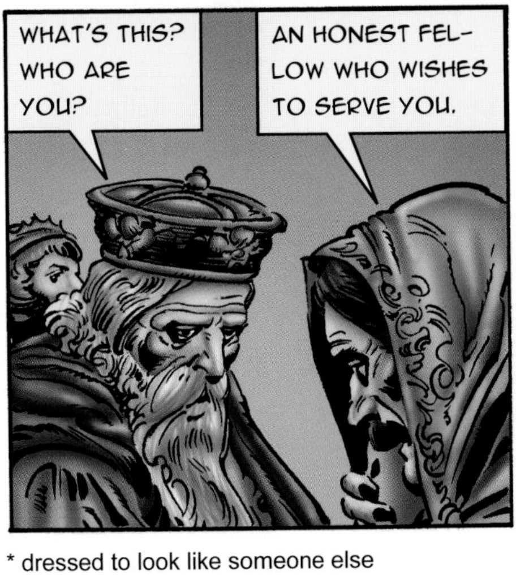
WHAT'S THIS? WHO ARE YOU?
AN HONEST FEL-LOW WHO WISHES TO SERVE YOU.

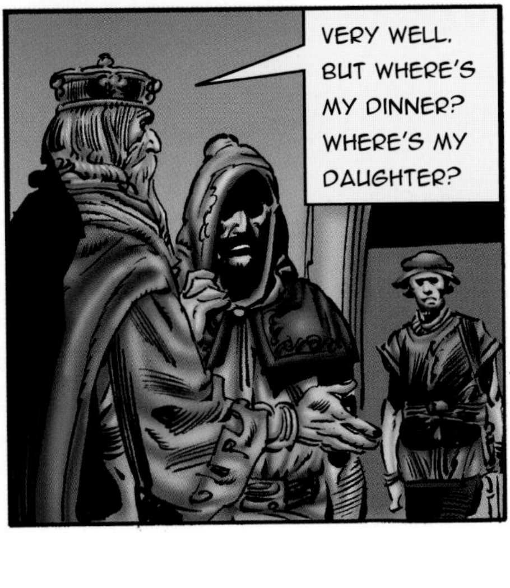
VERY WELL. BUT WHERE'S MY DINNER? WHERE'S MY DAUGHTER?

* dressed to look like someone else

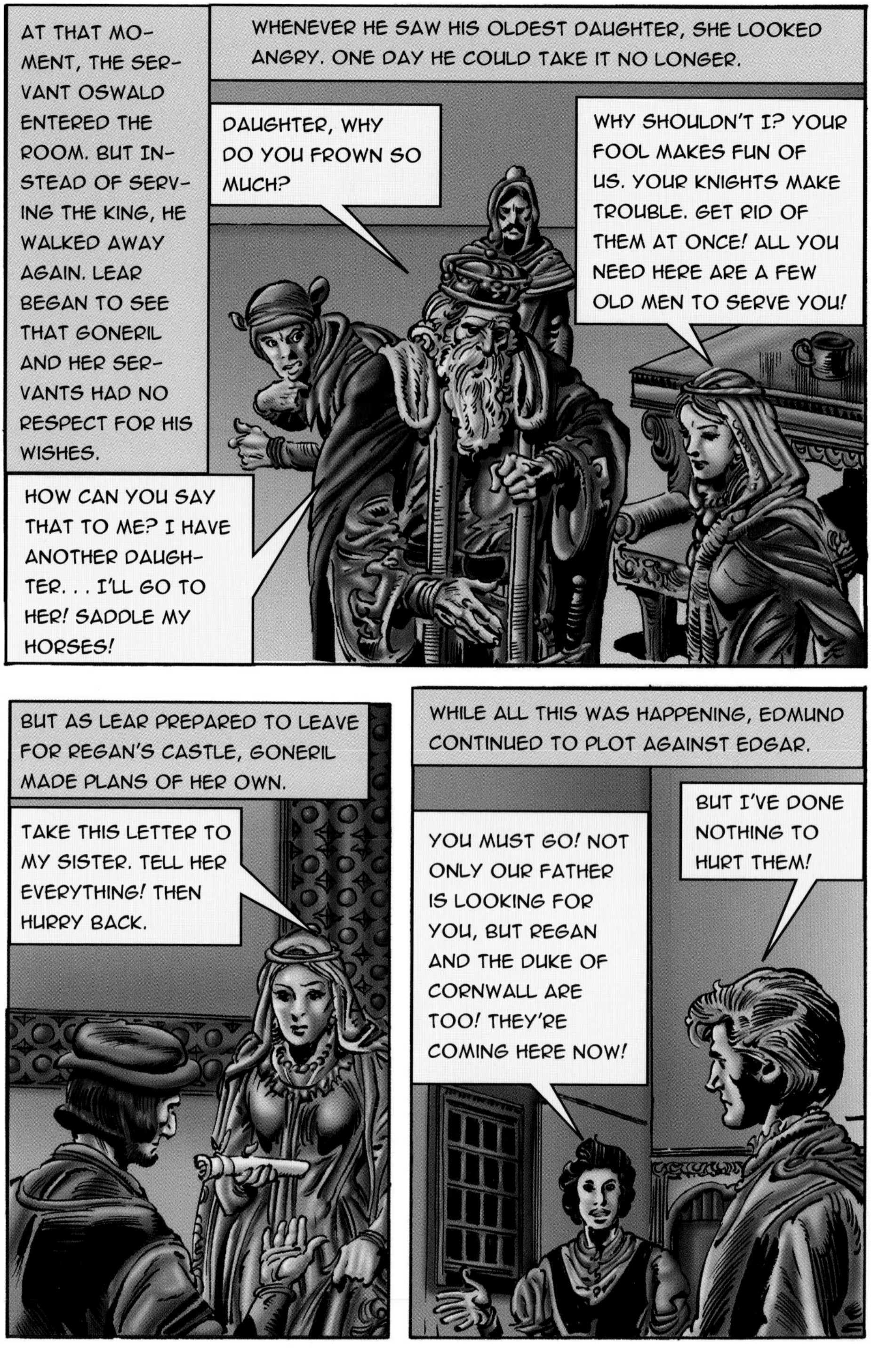
AT THAT MOMENT, THE SERVANT OSWALD ENTERED THE ROOM. BUT INSTEAD OF SERVING THE KING, HE WALKED AWAY AGAIN. LEAR BEGAN TO SEE THAT GONERIL AND HER SERVANTS HAD NO RESPECT FOR HIS WISHES.
WHENEVER HE SAW HIS OLDEST DAUGHTER, SHE LOOKED ANGRY. ONE DAY HE COULD TAKE IT NO LONGER.
DAUGHTER, WHY DO YOU FROWN SO MUCH?
WHY SHOULDN'T I? YOUR FOOL MAKES FUN OF US. YOUR KNIGHTS MAKE TROUBLE. GET RID OF THEM AT ONCE! ALL YOU NEED HERE ARE A FEW OLD MEN TO SERVE YOU!
HOW CAN YOU SAY THAT TO ME? I HAVE ANOTHER DAUGHTER. . . I'LL GO TO HER! SADDLE MY HORSES!
BUT AS LEAR PREPARED TO LEAVE FOR REGAN'S CASTLE, GONERIL MADE PLANS OF HER OWN.
TAKE THIS LETTER TO MY SISTER. TELL HER EVERYTHING! THEN HURRY BACK.
WHILE ALL THIS WAS HAPPENING, EDMUND CONTINUED TO PLOT AGAINST EDGAR.
YOU MUST GO! NOT ONLY OUR FATHER IS LOOKING FOR YOU, BUT REGAN AND THE DUKE OF CORNWALL ARE TOO! THEY'RE COMING HERE NOW!
BUT I'VE DONE NOTHING TO HURT THEM!

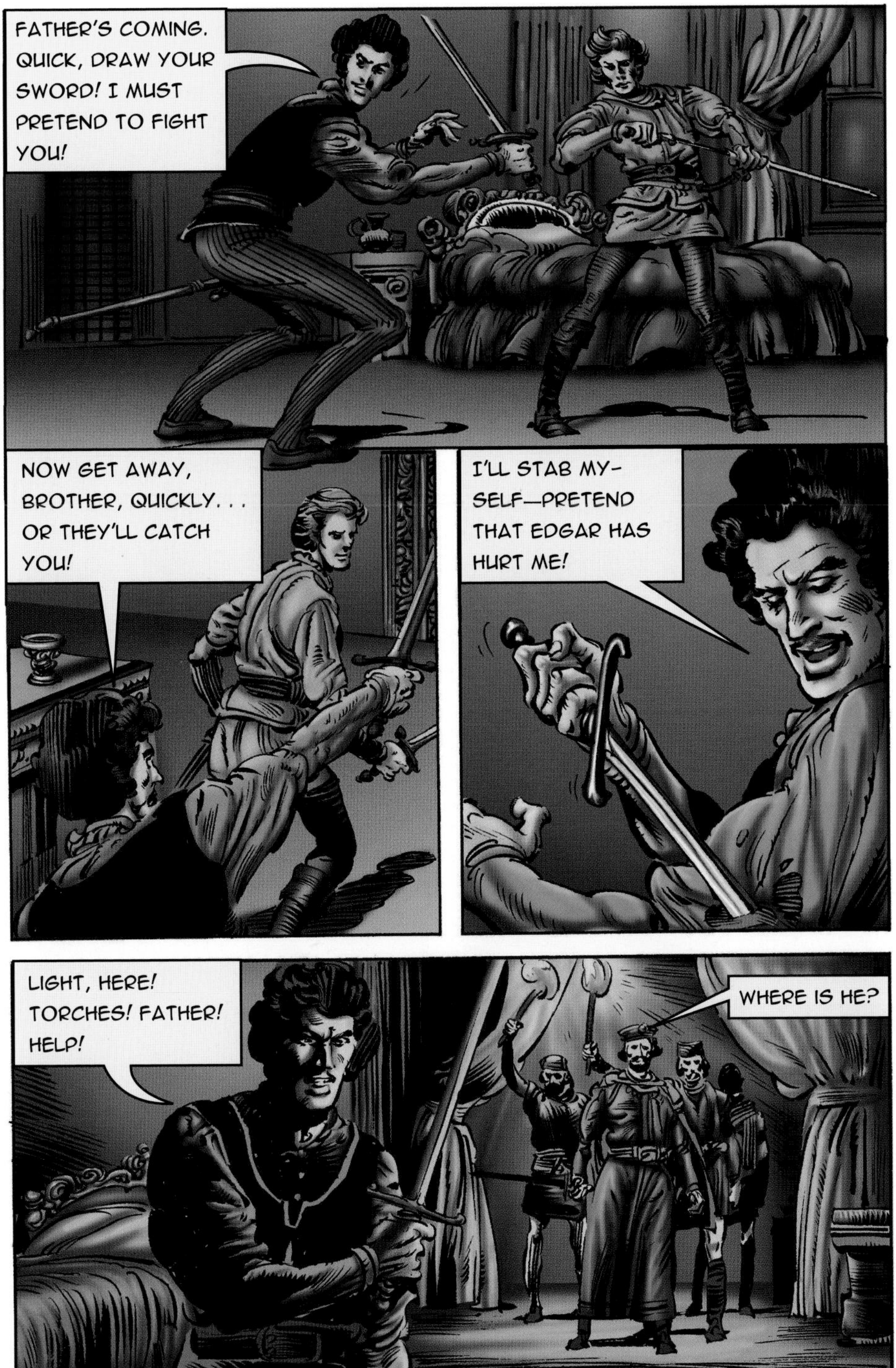
FATHER'S COMING. QUICK, DRAW YOUR SWORD! I MUST PRETEND TO FIGHT YOU!
NOW GET AWAY, BROTHER, QUICKLY. . . OR THEY'LL CATCH YOU!
I'LL STAB MY-SELF—PRETEND THAT EDGAR HAS HURT ME!
LIGHT, HERE! TORCHES! FATHER! HELP!
WHERE IS HE?

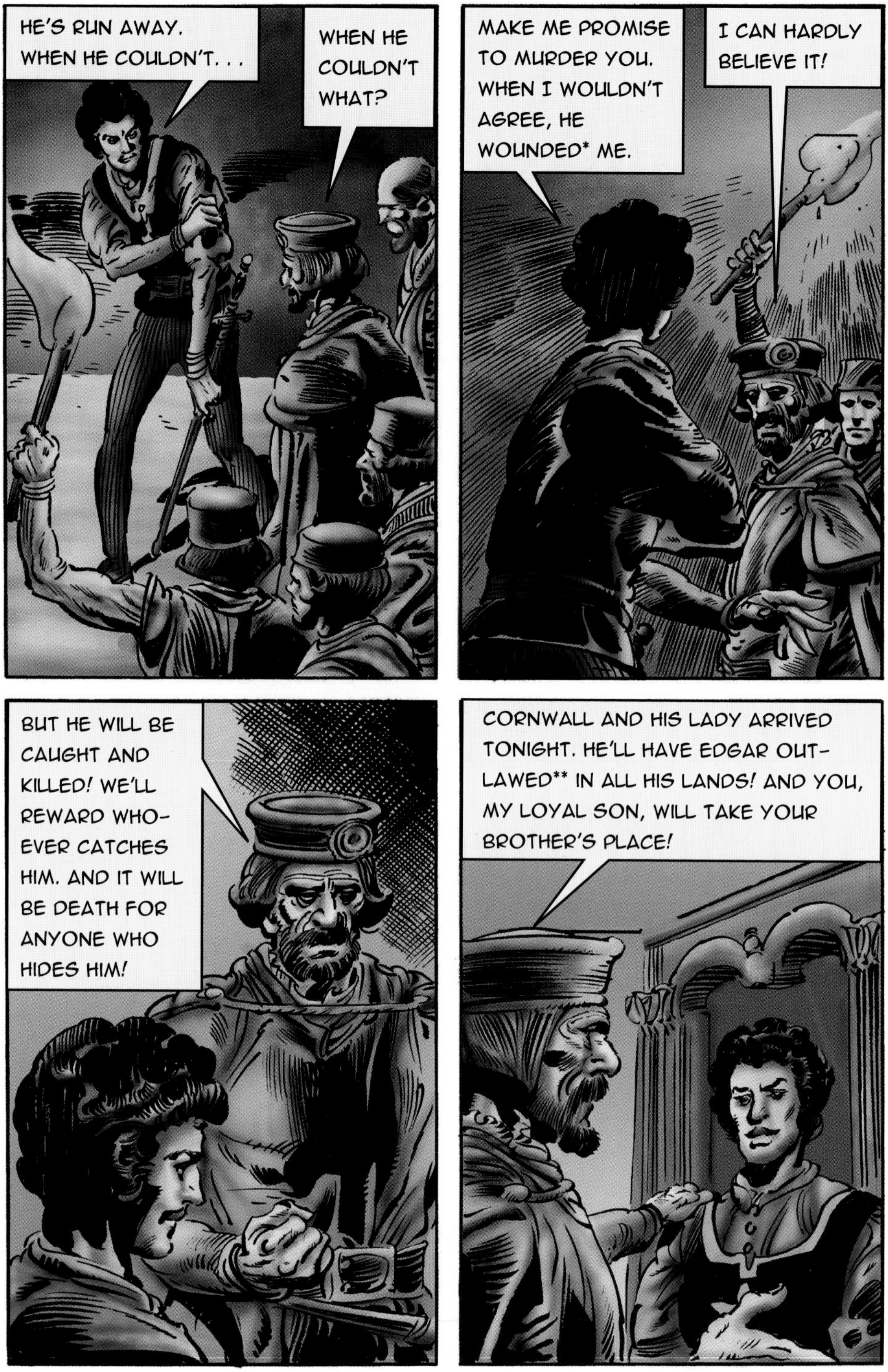
HE'S RUN AWAY. WHEN HE COULDN'T. . .
WHEN HE COULDN'T WHAT?
MAKE ME PROMISE TO MURDER YOU. WHEN I WOULDN'T AGREE, HE WOUNDED* ME.
I CAN HARDLY BELIEVE IT!
BUT HE WILL BE CAUGHT AND KILLED! WE'LL REWARD WHO-EVER CATCHES HIM. AND IT WILL BE DEATH FOR ANYONE WHO HIDES HIM!
CORNWALL AND HIS LADY ARRIVED TONIGHT. HE'LL HAVE EDGAR OUT-LAWED** IN ALL HIS LANDS! AND YOU, MY LOYAL SON, WILL TAKE YOUR BROTHER'S PLACE!

* injured, cut

** hunted as a criminal

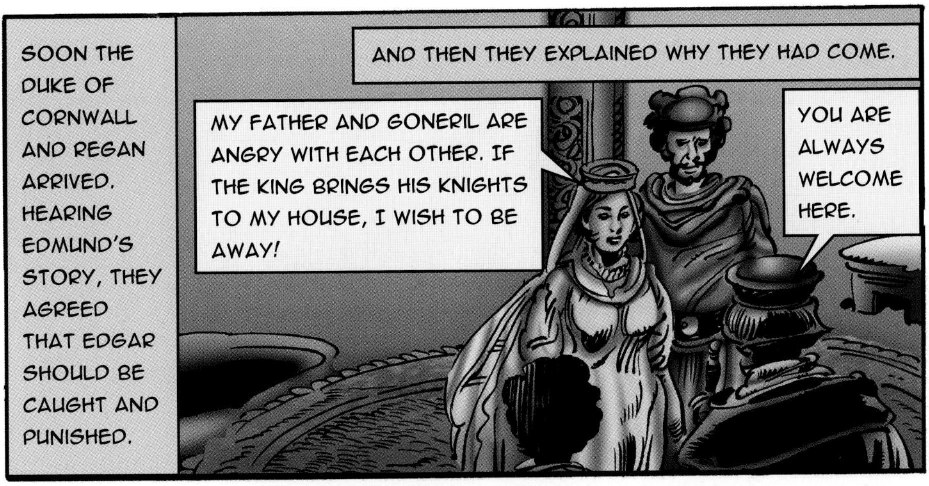
SOON THE DUKE OF CORNWALL AND REGAN ARRIVED. HEARING EDMUND'S STORY, THEY AGREED THAT EDGAR SHOULD BE CAUGHT AND PUNISHED.
AND THEN THEY EXPLAINED WHY THEY HAD COME.
MY FATHER AND GONERIL ARE ANGRY WITH EACH OTHER. IF THE KING BRINGS HIS KNIGHTS TO MY HOUSE, I WISH TO BE AWAY!
YOU ARE ALWAYS WELCOME HERE.

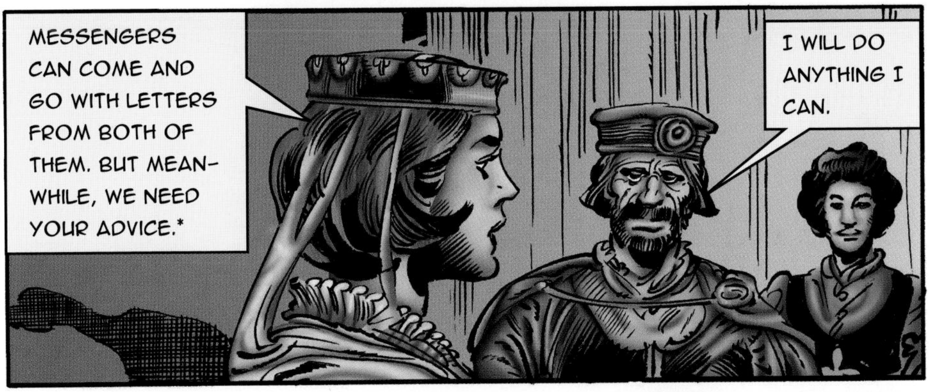
MESSENGERS CAN COME AND GO WITH LETTERS FROM BOTH OF THEM. BUT MEAN-WHILE, WE NEED YOUR ADVICE.*
I WILL DO ANYTHING I CAN.

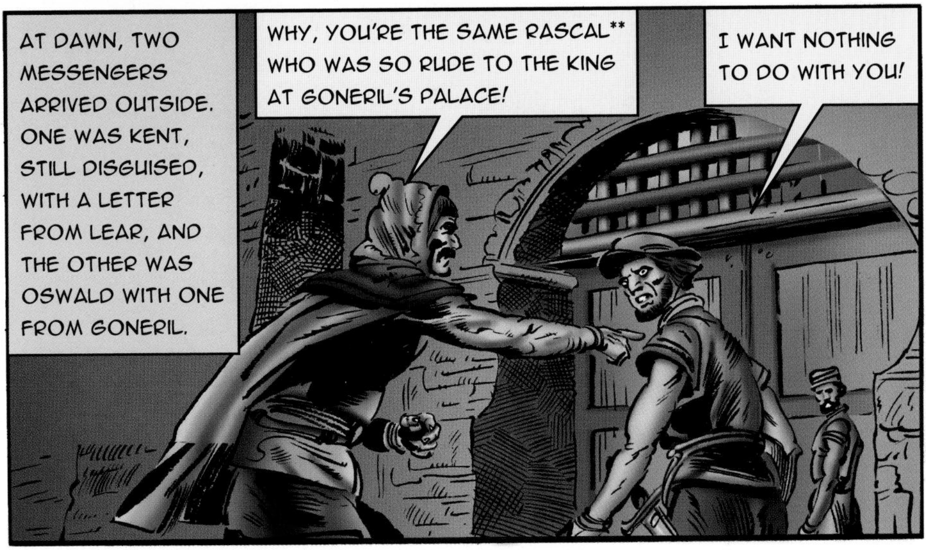
AT DAWN, TWO MESSENGERS ARRIVED OUTSIDE. ONE WAS KENT, STILL DISGUISED, WITH A LETTER FROM LEAR, AND THE OTHER WAS OSWALD WITH ONE FROM GONERIL.
WHY, YOU'RE THE SAME RASCAL** WHO WAS SO RUDE TO THE KING AT GONERIL'S PALACE!
I WANT NOTHING TO DO WITH YOU!

* help

** dishonest person

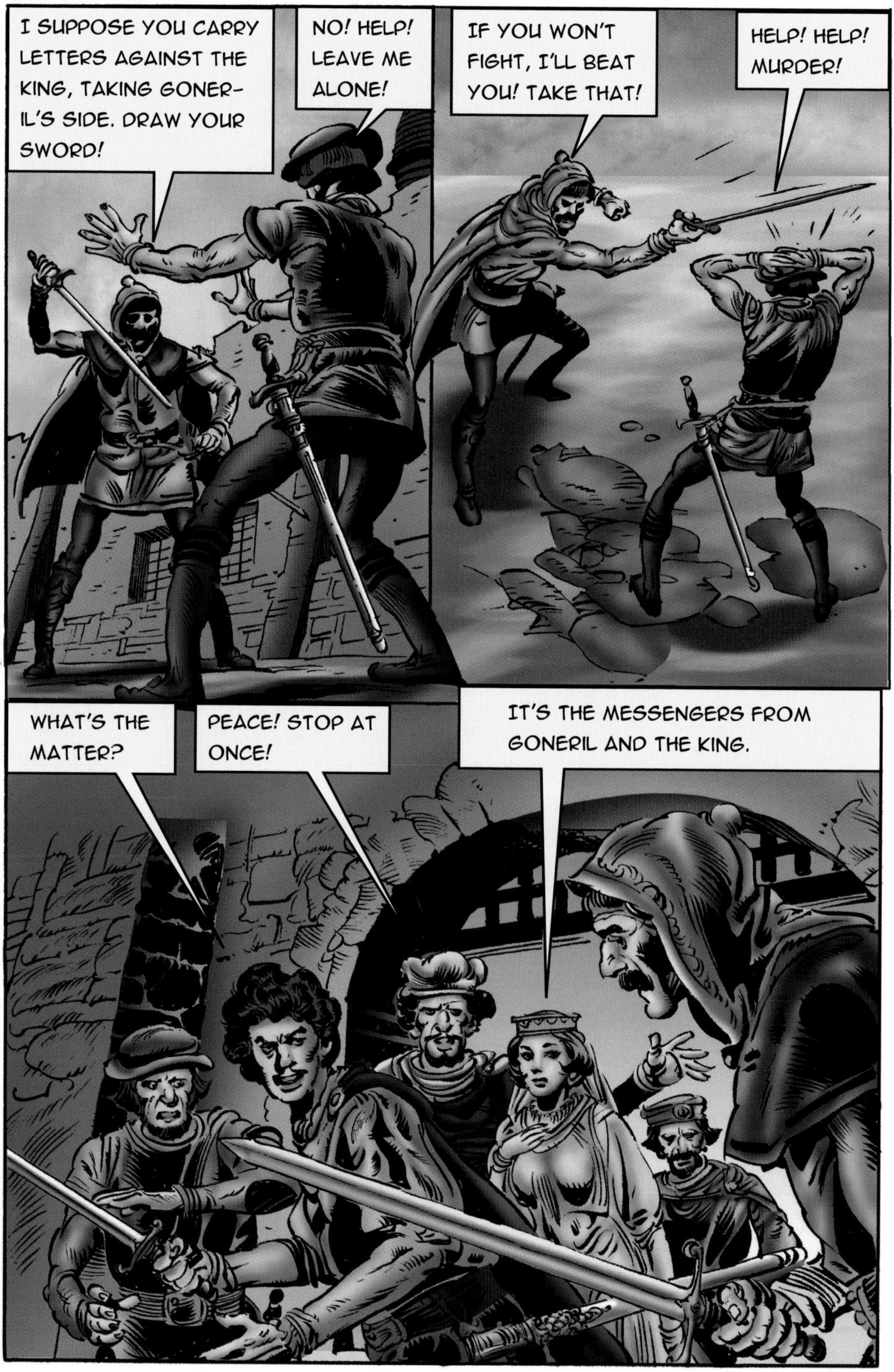
I SUPPOSE YOU CARRY LETTERS AGAINST THE KING, TAKING GONER-IL'S SIDE. DRAW YOUR SWORD!
NO! HELP! LEAVE ME ALONE!
IF YOU WON'T FIGHT, I'LL BEAT YOU! TAKE THAT!
HELP! HELP! MURDER!
WHAT'S THE MATTER?
PEACE! STOP AT ONCE!
IT'S THE MESSENGERS FROM GONERIL AND THE KING.

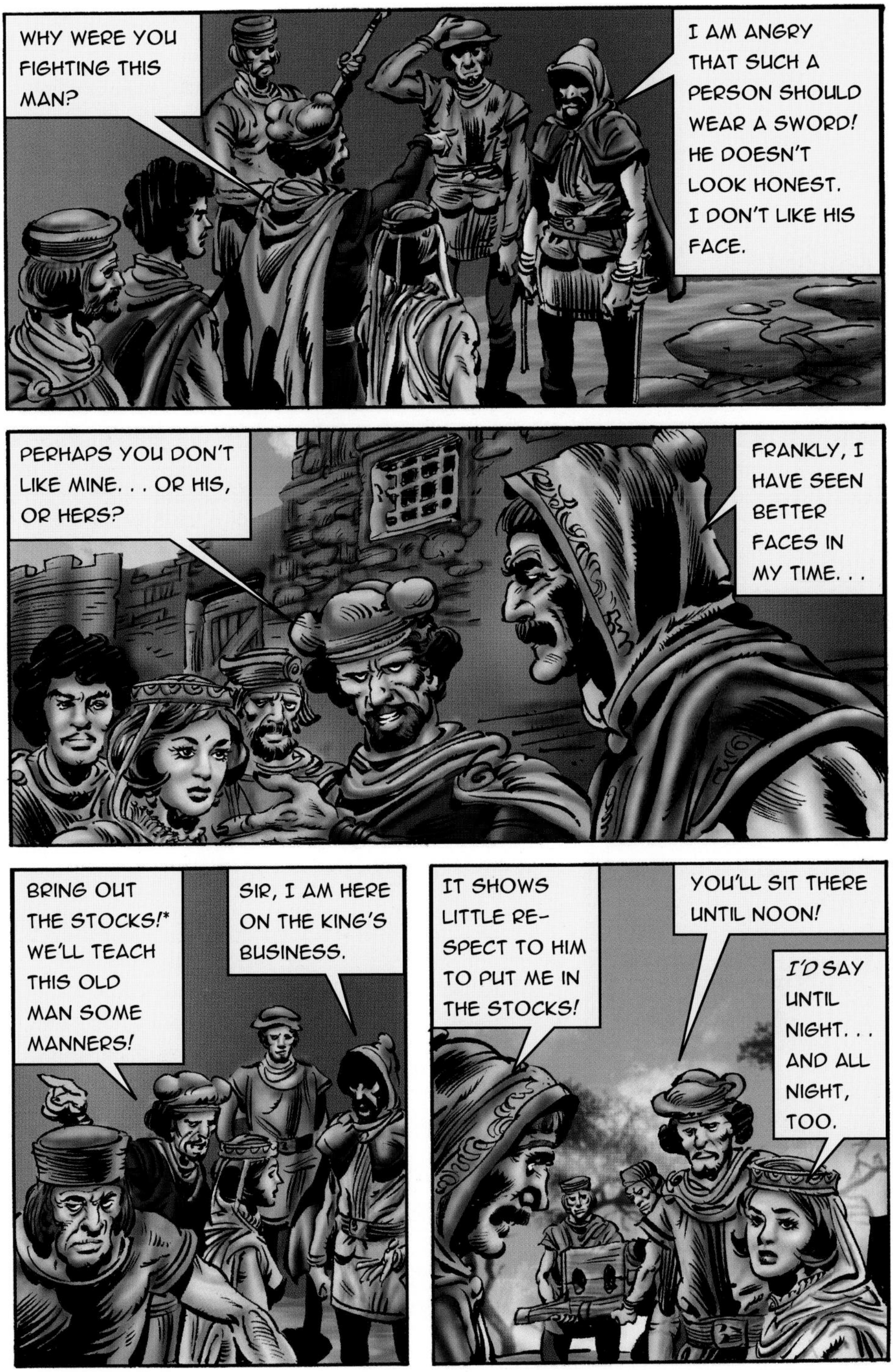
WHY WERE YOU FIGHTING THIS MAN?
I AM ANGRY THAT SUCH A PERSON SHOULD WEAR A SWORD! HE DOESN'T LOOK HONEST. I DON'T LIKE HIS FACE.
PERHAPS YOU DON'T LIKE MINE. . . OR HIS, OR HERS?
FRANKLY, I HAVE SEEN BETTER FACES IN MY TIME. . .
BRING OUT THE STOCKS!* WE'LL TEACH THIS OLD MAN SOME MANNERS!
SIR, I AM HERE ON THE KING'S BUSINESS.
IT SHOWS LITTLE RE-SPECT TO HIM TO PUT ME IN THE STOCKS!
YOU'LL SIT THERE UNTIL NOON!
I'D SAY UNTIL NIGHT. . . AND ALL NIGHT, TOO.

* a wooden frame in which a person to be punished must sit for a certain time

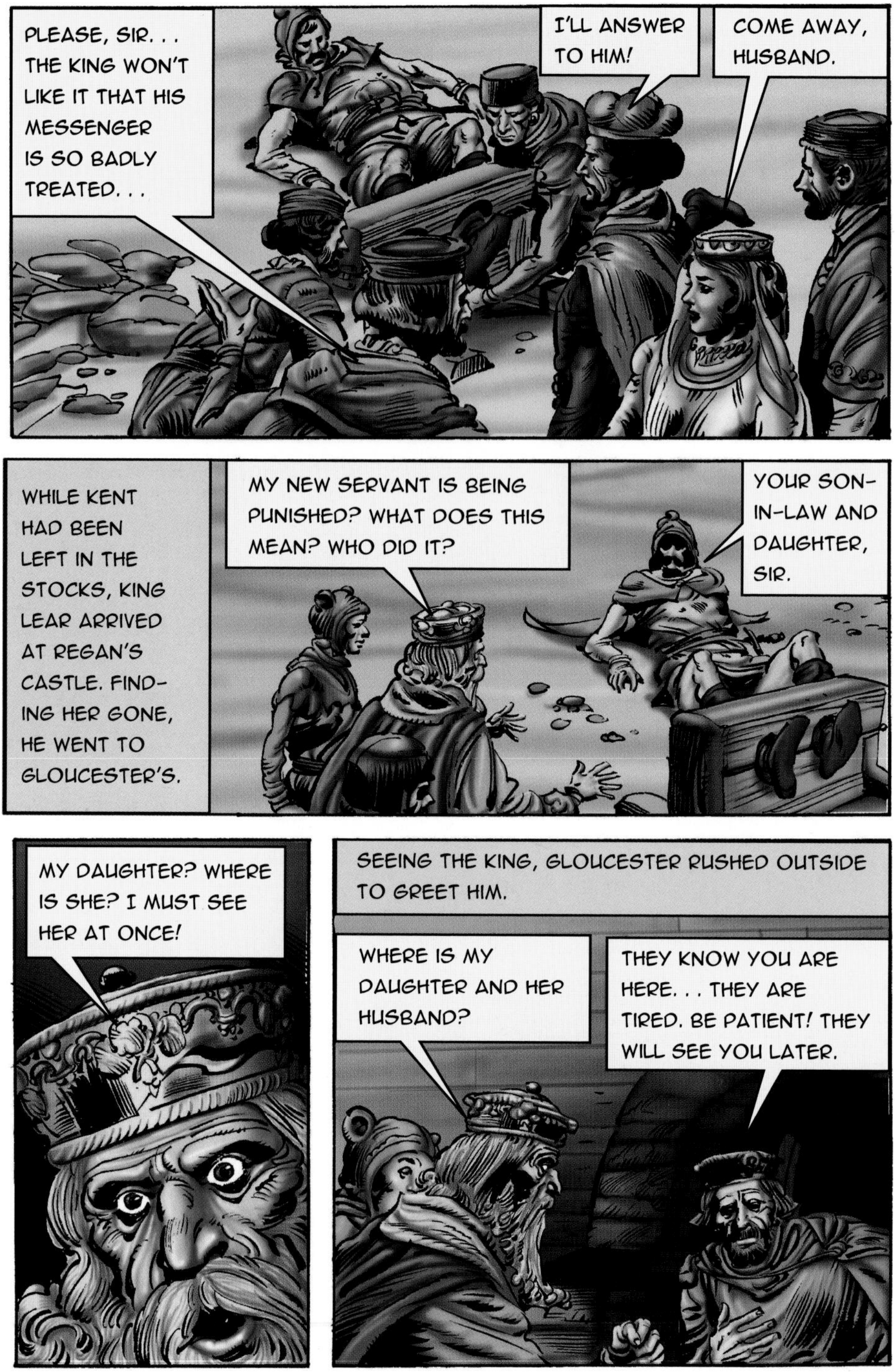
PLEASE, SIR. . . THE KING WON'T LIKE IT THAT HIS MESSENGER IS SO BADLY TREATED. . .
I'LL ANSWER TO HIM!
COME AWAY, HUSBAND.
WHILE KENT HAD BEEN LEFT IN THE STOCKS, KING LEAR ARRIVED AT REGAN'S CASTLE. FINDING HER GONE, HE WENT TO GLOUCESTER'S.
MY NEW SERVANT IS BEING PUNISHED? WHAT DOES THIS MEAN? WHO DID IT?
YOUR SON-IN-LAW AND DAUGHTER, SIR.
MY DAUGHTER? WHERE IS SHE? I MUST SEE HER AT ONCE!
SEEING THE KING, GLOUCESTER RUSHED OUTSIDE TO GREET HIM.
WHERE IS MY DAUGHTER AND HER HUSBAND?
THEY KNOW YOU ARE HERE. . . THEY ARE TIRED. BE PATIENT! THEY WILL SEE YOU LATER.

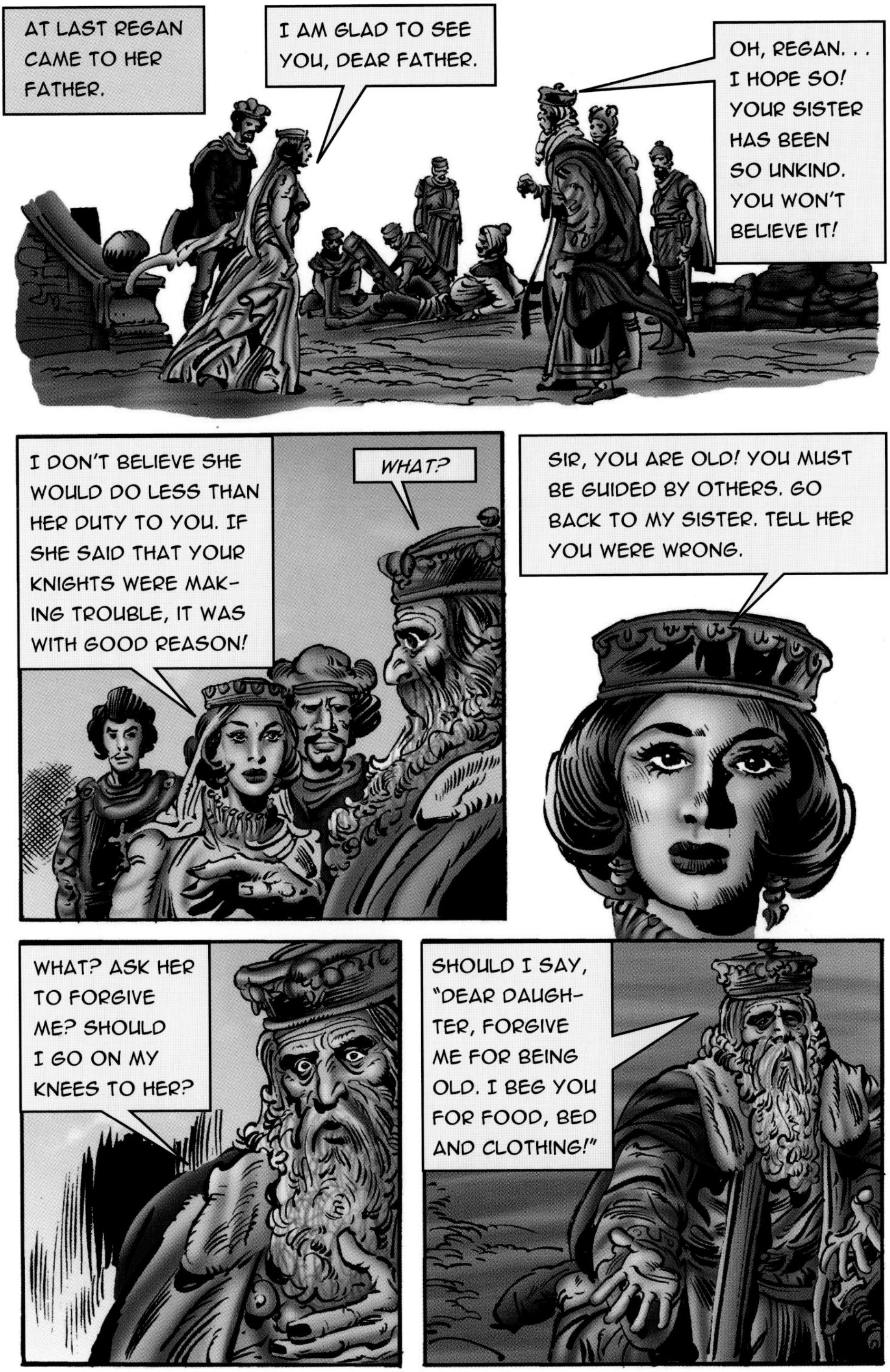
AT LAST REGAN CAME TO HER FATHER.
I AM GLAD TO SEE YOU, DEAR FATHER.
OH, REGAN. . . I HOPE SO! YOUR SISTER HAS BEEN SO UNKIND. YOU WON'T BELIEVE IT!
I DON'T BELIEVE SHE WOULD DO LESS THAN HER DUTY TO YOU. IF SHE SAID THAT YOUR KNIGHTS WERE MAKING TROUBLE, IT WAS WITH GOOD REASON!
WHAT?
SIR, YOU ARE OLD! YOU MUST BE GUIDED BY OTHERS. GO BACK TO MY SISTER. TELL HER YOU WERE WRONG.
WHAT? ASK HER TO FORGIVE ME? SHOULD I GO ON MY KNEES TO HER?
SHOULD I SAY, "DEAR DAUGHTER, FORGIVE ME FOR BEING OLD. I BEG YOU FOR FOOD, BED AND CLOTHING!"

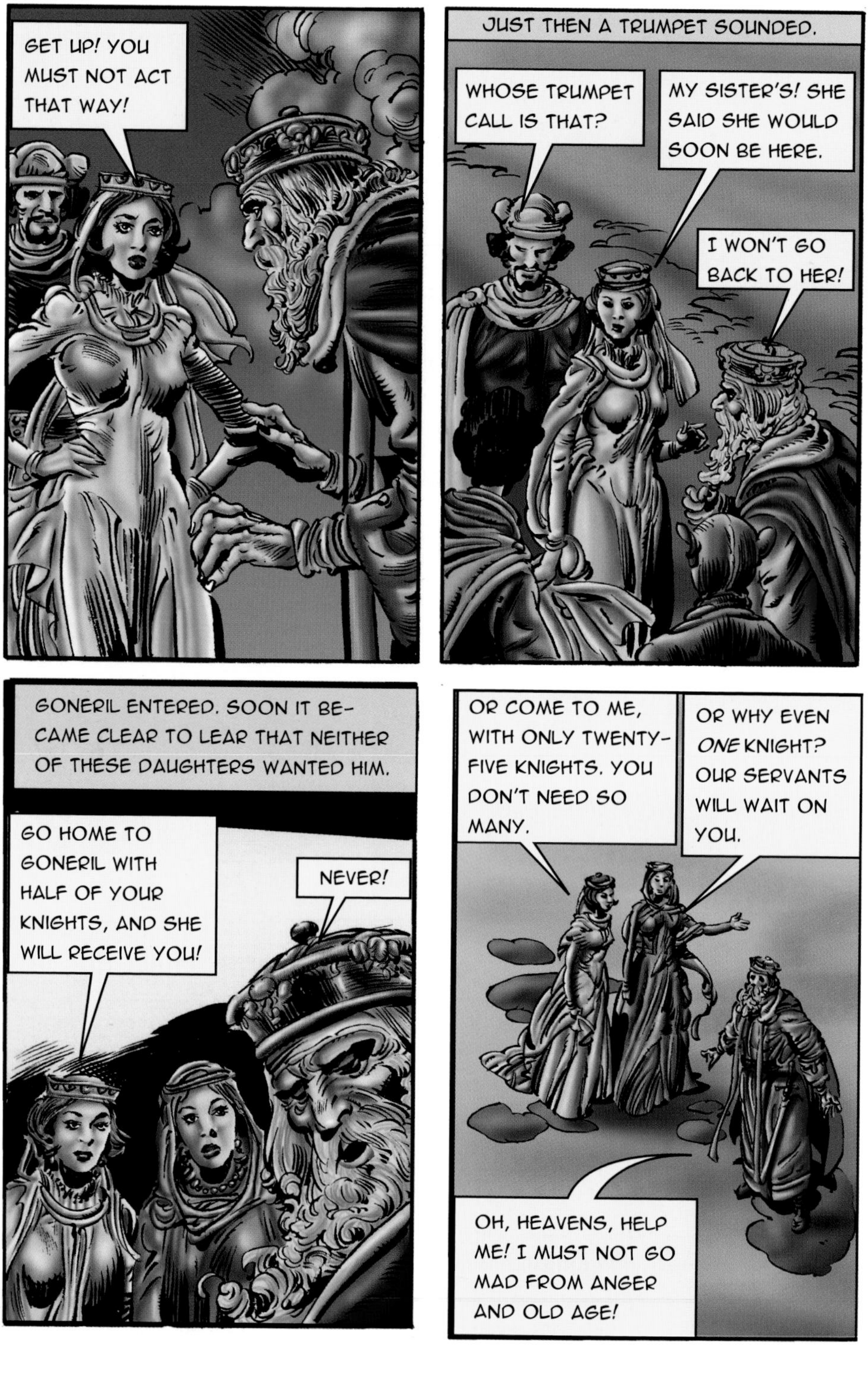
GET UP! YOU MUST NOT ACT THAT WAY!
JUST THEN A TRUMPET SOUNDED.
WHOSE TRUMPET CALL IS THAT?
MY SISTER'S! SHE SAID SHE WOULD SOON BE HERE.
I WON'T GO BACK TO HER!
GONERIL ENTERED. SOON IT BECAME CLEAR TO LEAR THAT NEITHER OF THESE DAUGHTERS WANTED HIM.
GO HOME TO GONERIL WITH HALF OF YOUR KNIGHTS, AND SHE WILL RECEIVE YOU!
NEVER!
OR COME TO ME, WITH ONLY TWENTY-FIVE KNIGHTS. YOU DON'T NEED SO MANY.
OR WHY EVEN ONE KNIGHT? OUR SERVANTS WILL WAIT ON YOU.
OH, HEAVENS, HELP ME! I MUST NOT GO MAD FROM ANGER AND OLD AGE!

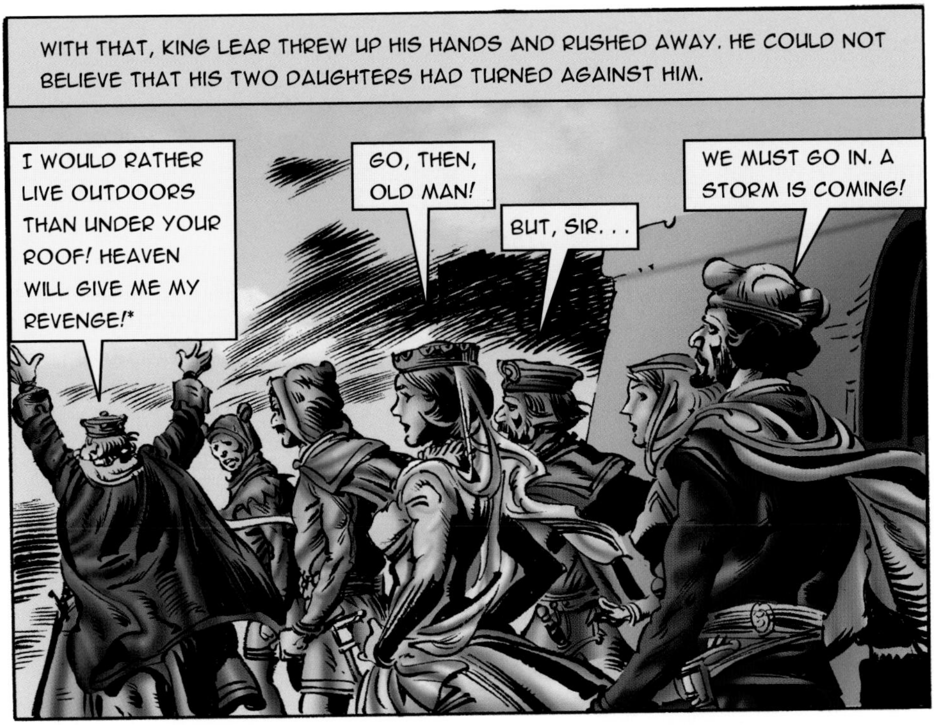
WITH THAT, KING LEAR THREW UP HIS HANDS AND RUSHED AWAY. HE COULD NOT BELIEVE THAT HIS TWO DAUGHTERS HAD TURNED AGAINST HIM.
I WOULD RATHER LIVE OUTDOORS THAN UNDER YOUR ROOF! HEAVEN WILL GIVE ME MY REVENGE!*
GO, THEN, OLD MAN!
BUT, SIR. . .
WE MUST GO IN. A STORM IS COMING!

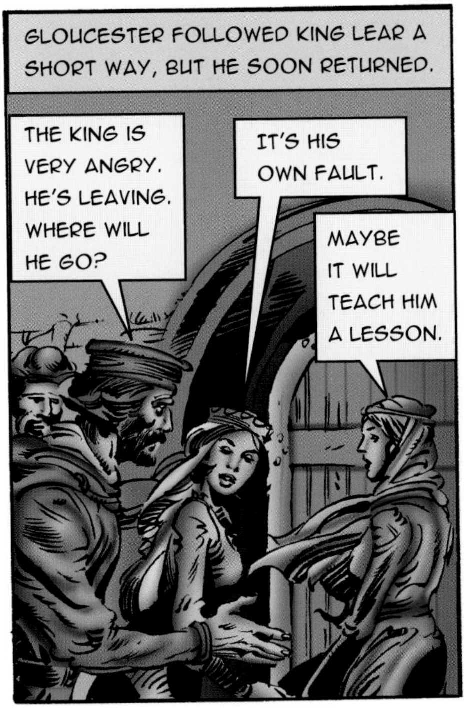
GLOUCESTER FOLLOWED KING LEAR A SHORT WAY, BUT HE SOON RETURNED.
THE KING IS VERY ANGRY. HE'S LEAVING. WHERE WILL HE GO?
IT'S HIS OWN FAULT.
MAYBE IT WILL TEACH HIM A LESSON.

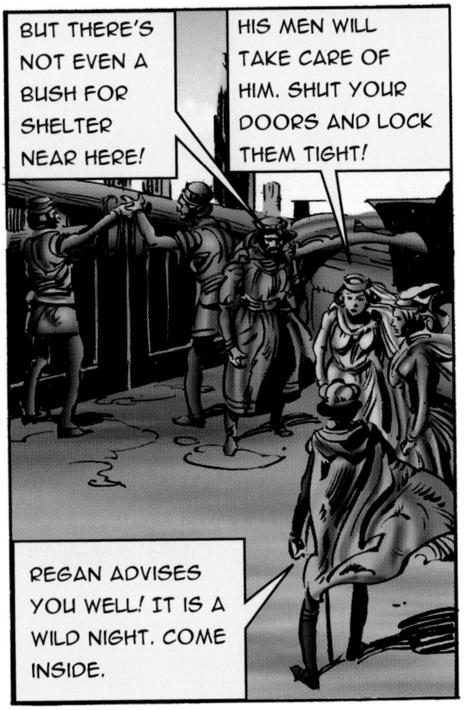
BUT THERE'S NOT EVEN A BUSH FOR SHELTER NEAR HERE!
HIS MEN WILL TAKE CARE OF HIM. SHUT YOUR DOORS AND LOCK THEM TIGHT!
REGAN ADVISES YOU WELL! IT IS A WILD NIGHT. COME INSIDE.

* getting even with someone

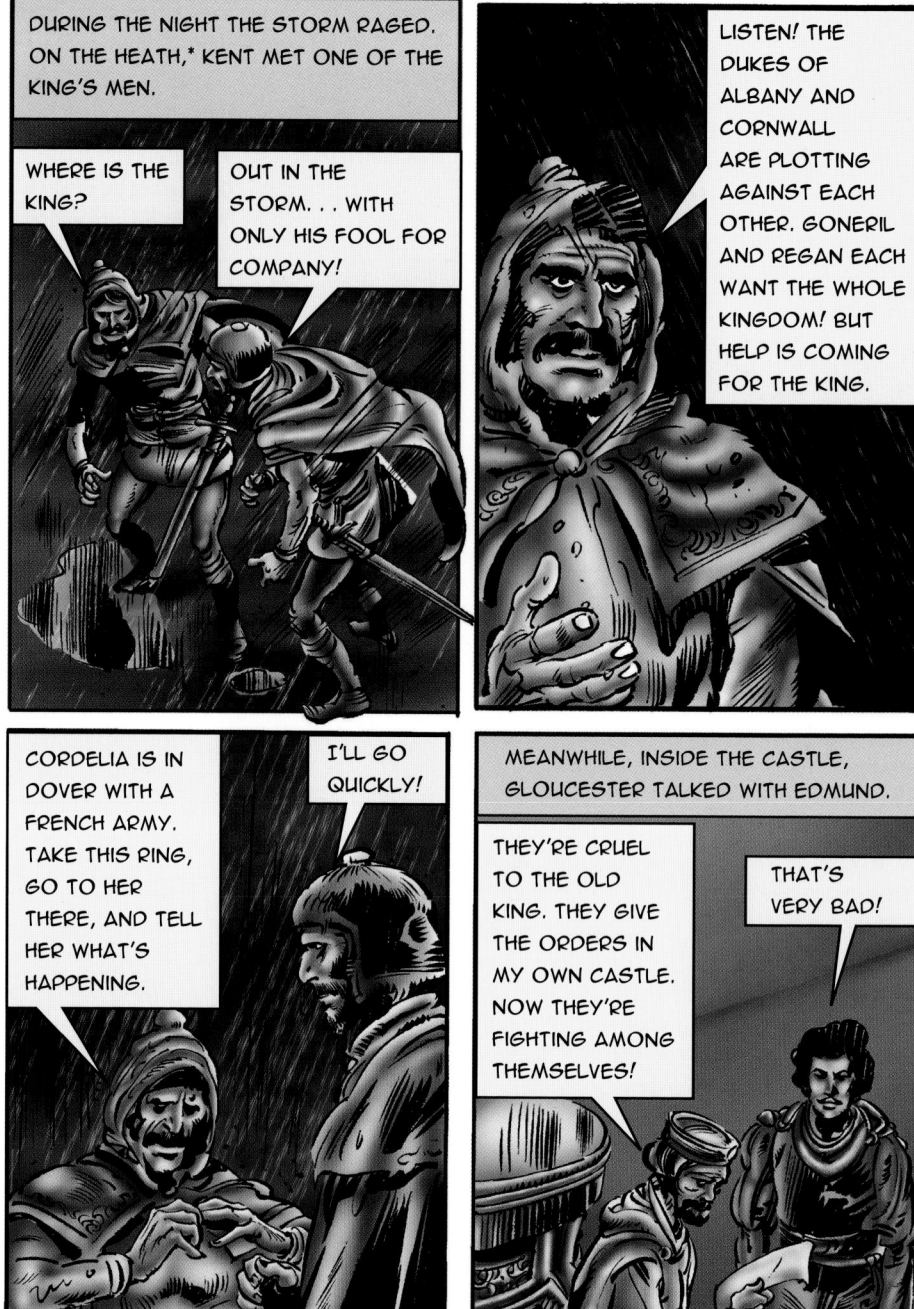

DURING THE NIGHT THE STORM RAGED. ON THE HEATH,* KENT MET ONE OF THE KING'S MEN.

WHERE IS THE KING?

OUT IN THE STORM. . . WITH ONLY HIS FOOL FOR COMPANY!

LISTEN! THE DUKES OF ALBANY AND CORNWALL ARE PLOTTING AGAINST EACH OTHER. GONERIL AND REGAN EACH WANT THE WHOLE KINGDOM! BUT HELP IS COMING FOR THE KING.

CORDELIA IS IN DOVER WITH A FRENCH ARMY. TAKE THIS RING, GO TO HER THERE, AND TELL HER WHAT'S HAPPENING.

I'LL GO QUICKLY!

MEANWHILE, INSIDE THE CASTLE, GLOUCESTER TALKED WITH EDMUND.

THEY'RE CRUEL TO THE OLD KING. THEY GIVE THE ORDERS IN MY OWN CASTLE. NOW THEY'RE FIGHTING AMONG THEMSELVES!

THAT'S VERY BAD!

* a wild, marshy area

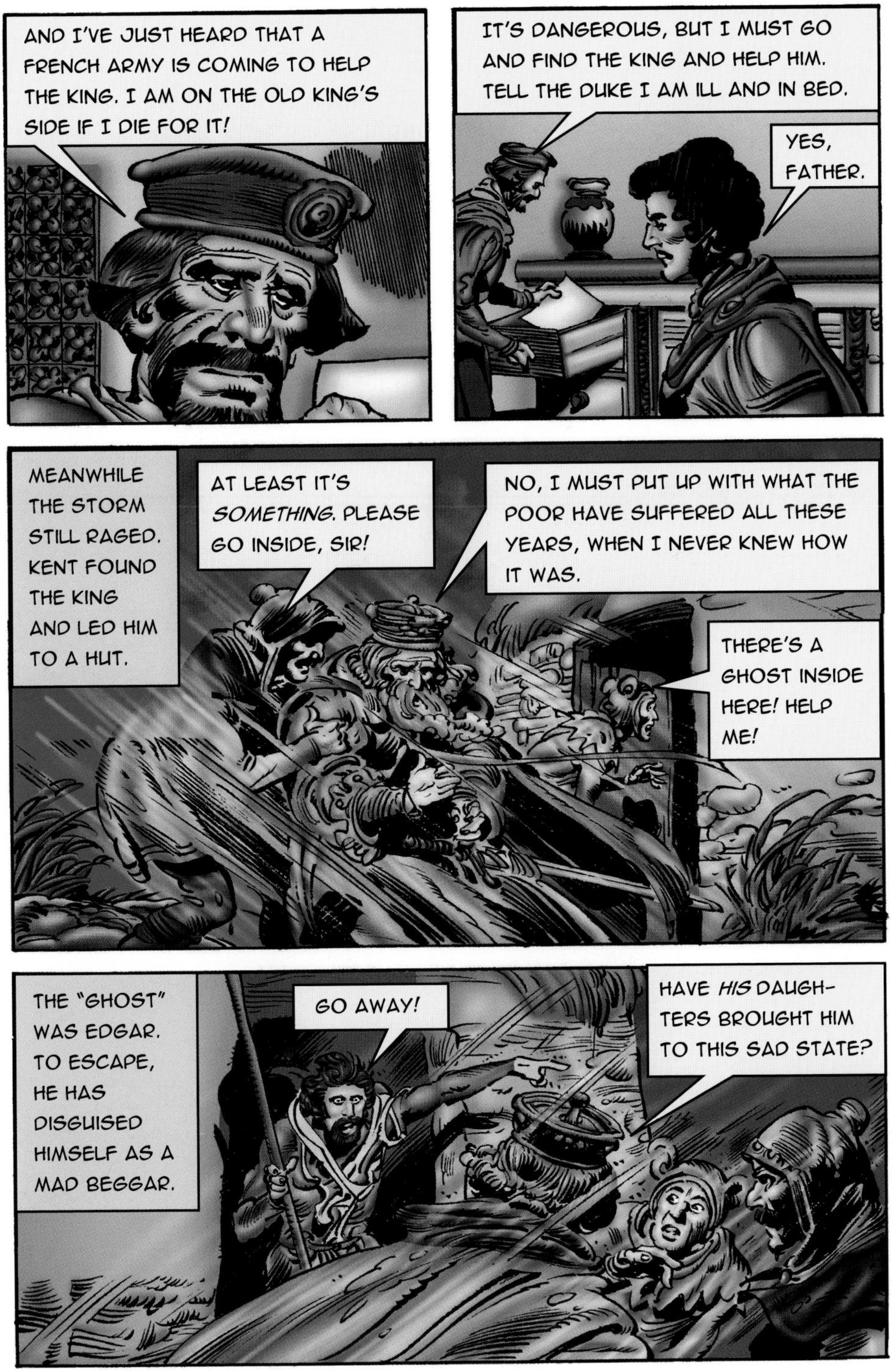
AND I'VE JUST HEARD THAT A FRENCH ARMY IS COMING TO HELP THE KING. I AM ON THE OLD KING'S SIDE IF I DIE FOR IT!
IT'S DANGEROUS, BUT I MUST GO AND FIND THE KING AND HELP HIM. TELL THE DUKE I AM ILL AND IN BED.
YES, FATHER.
MEANWHILE THE STORM STILL RAGED. KENT FOUND THE KING AND LED HIM TO A HUT.
AT LEAST IT'S *SOMETHING*. PLEASE GO INSIDE, SIR!
NO, I MUST PUT UP WITH WHAT THE POOR HAVE SUFFERED ALL THESE YEARS, WHEN I NEVER KNEW HOW IT WAS.
THERE'S A GHOST INSIDE HERE! HELP ME!
THE "GHOST" WAS EDGAR. TO ESCAPE, HE HAS DISGUISED HIMSELF AS A MAD BEGGAR.
GO AWAY!
HAVE *HIS* DAUGHTERS BROUGHT HIM TO THIS SAD STATE?

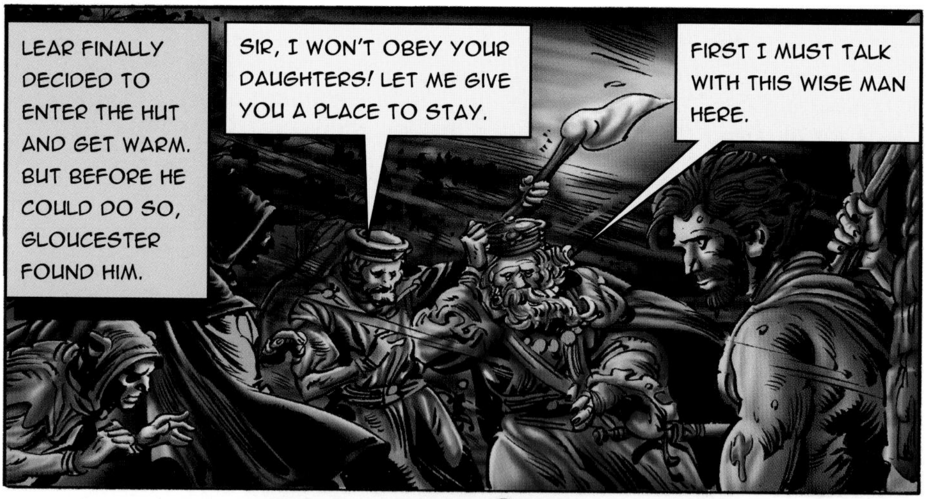
LEAR FINALLY DECIDED TO ENTER THE HUT AND GET WARM. BUT BEFORE HE COULD DO SO, GLOUCESTER FOUND HIM.
SIR, I WON'T OBEY YOUR DAUGHTERS! LET ME GIVE YOU A PLACE TO STAY.
FIRST I MUST TALK WITH THIS WISE MAN HERE.

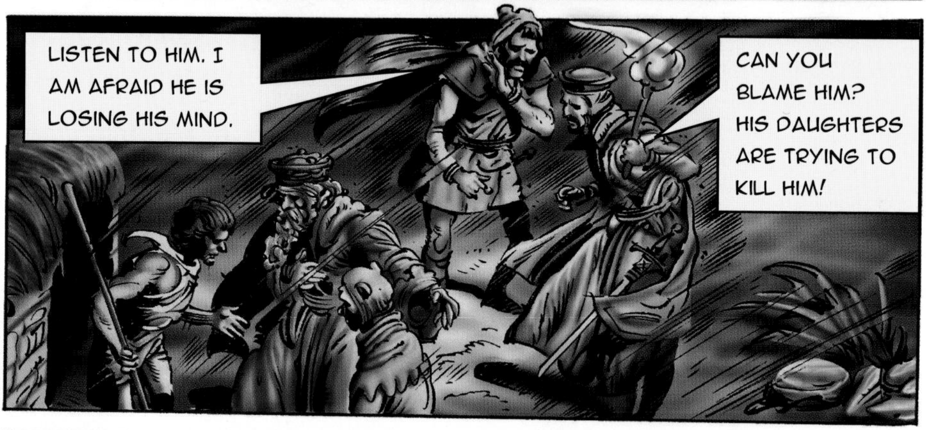
LISTEN TO HIM. I AM AFRAID HE IS LOSING HIS MIND.
CAN YOU BLAME HIM? HIS DAUGHTERS ARE TRYING TO KILL HIM!

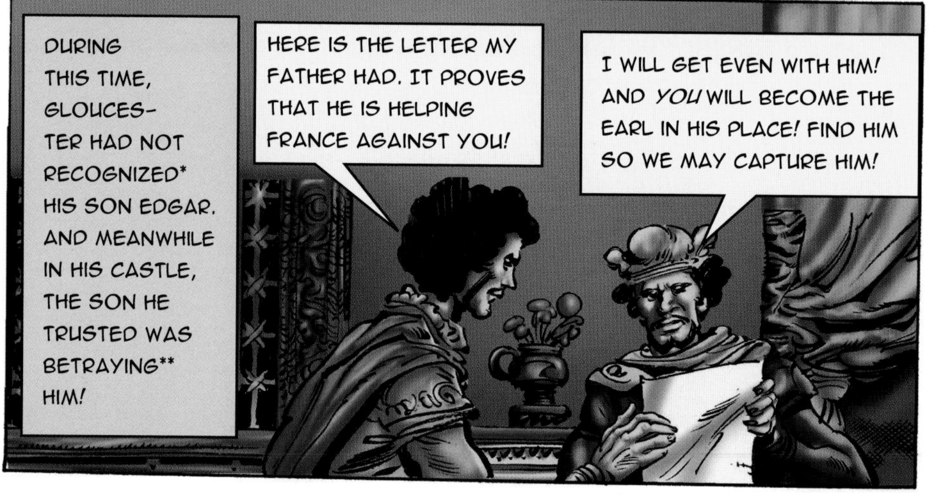
DURING THIS TIME, GLOUCES-TER HAD NOT RECOGNIZED* HIS SON EDGAR. AND MEANWHILE IN HIS CASTLE, THE SON HE TRUSTED WAS BETRAYING** HIM!
HERE IS THE LETTER MY FATHER HAD. IT PROVES THAT HE IS HELPING FRANCE AGAINST YOU!
I WILL GET EVEN WITH HIM! AND *YOU* WILL BECOME THE EARL IN HIS PLACE! FIND HIM SO WE MAY CAPTURE HIM!

* knew from seeing someone before

** doing evil to someone who trusts him

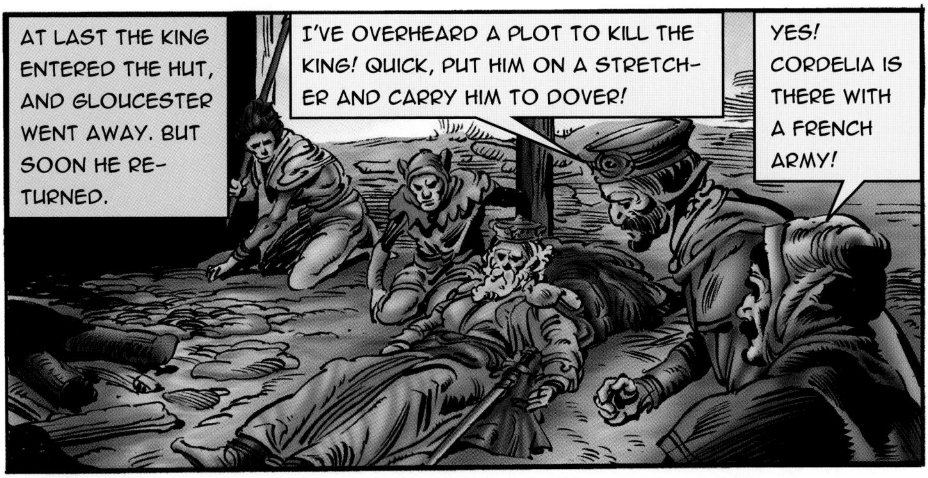
AT LAST THE KING ENTERED THE HUT, AND GLOUCESTER WENT AWAY. BUT SOON HE RE- TURNED.
I'VE OVERHEARD A PLOT TO KILL THE KING! QUICK, PUT HIM ON A STRETCH- ER AND CARRY HIM TO DOVER!
YES! CORDELIA IS THERE WITH A FRENCH ARMY!

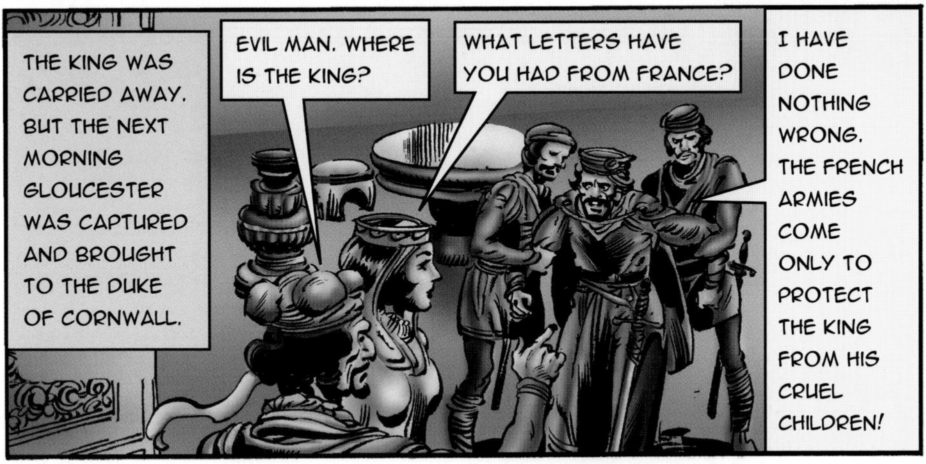
THE KING WAS CARRIED AWAY. BUT THE NEXT MORNING GLOUCESTER WAS CAPTURED AND BROUGHT TO THE DUKE OF CORNWALL.
EVIL MAN. WHERE IS THE KING?
WHAT LETTERS HAVE YOU HAD FROM FRANCE?
I HAVE DONE NOTHING WRONG. THE FRENCH ARMIES COME ONLY TO PROTECT THE KING FROM HIS CRUEL CHILDREN!

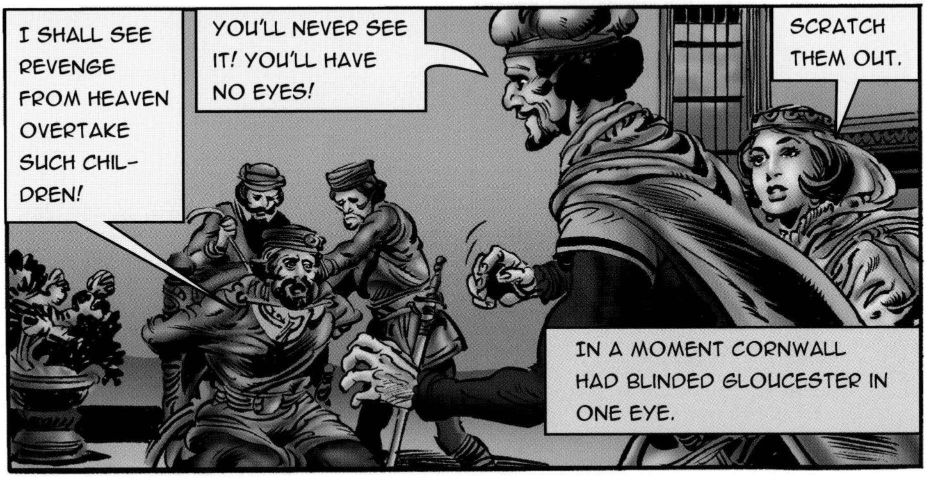
I SHALL SEE REVENGE FROM HEAVEN OVERTAKE SUCH CHIL- DREN!
YOU'LL NEVER SEE IT! YOU'LL HAVE NO EYES!
SCRATCH THEM OUT.
IN A MOMENT CORNWALL HAD BLINDED GLOUCESTER IN ONE EYE.

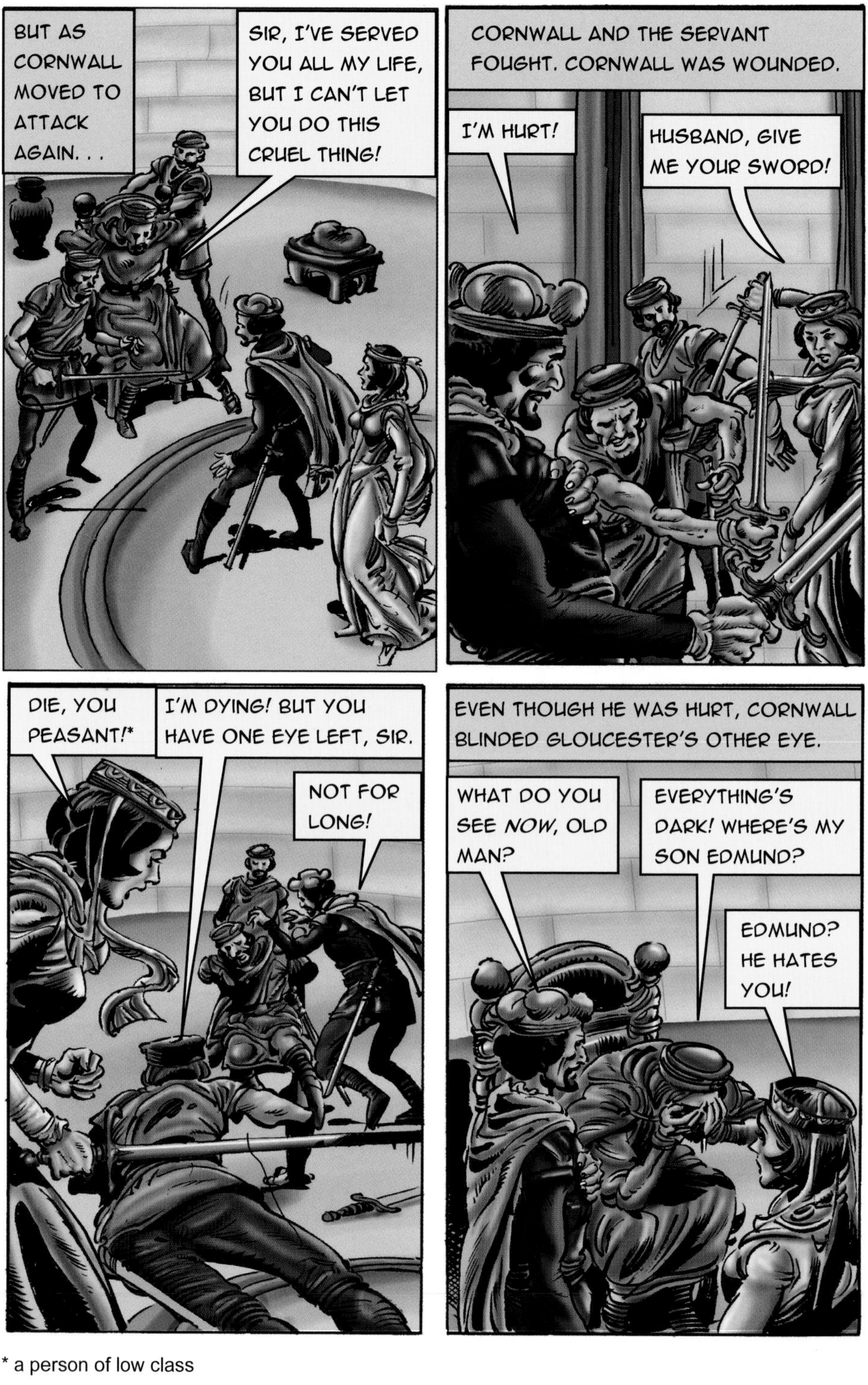
BUT AS CORNWALL MOVED TO ATTACK AGAIN. . .
SIR, I'VE SERVED YOU ALL MY LIFE, BUT I CAN'T LET YOU DO THIS CRUEL THING!
CORNWALL AND THE SERVANT FOUGHT. CORNWALL WAS WOUNDED.
I'M HURT!
HUSBAND, GIVE ME YOUR SWORD!
DIE, YOU PEASANT!*
I'M DYING! BUT YOU HAVE ONE EYE LEFT, SIR.
NOT FOR LONG!
EVEN THOUGH HE WAS HURT, CORNWALL BLINDED GLOUCESTER'S OTHER EYE.
WHAT DO YOU SEE *NOW*, OLD MAN?
EVERYTHING'S DARK! WHERE'S MY SON EDMUND?
EDMUND? HE HATES YOU!

* a person of low class

IT WAS ED-MUND WHO SHOWED US THE LETTER YOU HAD!

THEN EDGAR HAS BEEN TRUE TO ME!

PUT GLOUCESTER OUTSIDE THE GATES. LET HIM SMELL HIS WAY TO DOVER.

HELP ME REGAN. I'M BADLY HURT!

YOU MUST LEAVE ME, FRIEND, FOR YOU'LL BE IN TROUBLE! BUT WHO IS HERE?

IT'S, TOM THE MAD MAN.

GLOUCESTER WAS PUT OUTSIDE. A VERY OLD MAN CAME BY AND HELPED HIM. SOON THEY MET EDGAR, STILL DRESSED LIKE A MAD BEGGAR.

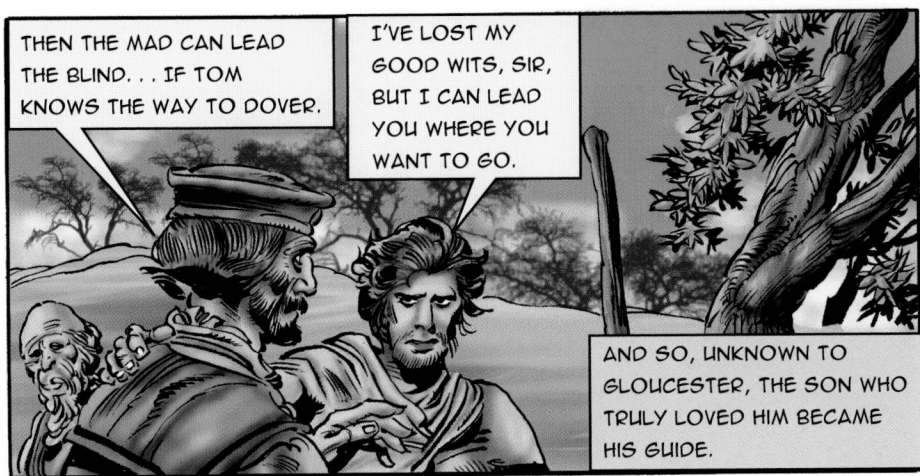

THEN THE MAD CAN LEAD THE BLIND. . . IF TOM KNOWS THE WAY TO DOVER.

I'VE LOST MY GOOD WITS, SIR, BUT I CAN LEAD YOU WHERE YOU WANT TO GO.

AND SO, UNKNOWN TO GLOUCESTER, THE SON WHO TRULY LOVED HIM BECAME HIS GUIDE.

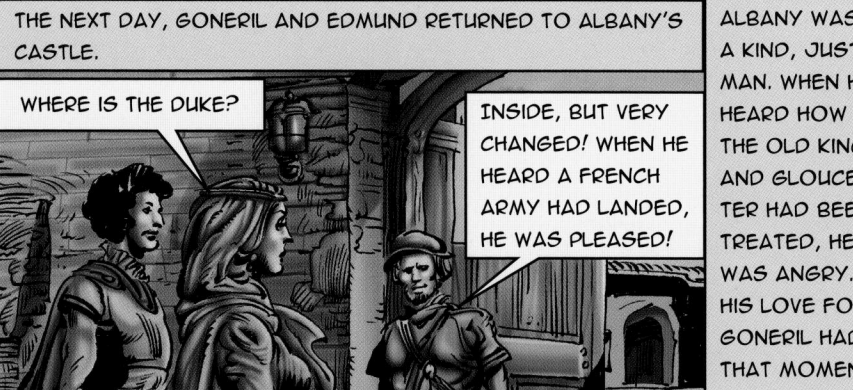

THE NEXT DAY, GONERIL AND EDMUND RETURNED TO ALBANY'S CASTLE.

WHERE IS THE DUKE?

INSIDE, BUT VERY CHANGED! WHEN HE HEARD A FRENCH ARMY HAD LANDED, HE WAS PLEASED!

ALBANY WAS A KIND, JUST MAN. WHEN HE HEARD HOW THE OLD KING AND GLOUCESTER HAD BEEN TREATED, HE WAS ANGRY. HIS LOVE FOR GONERIL HAD THAT MOMENT TURNED TO HATE.

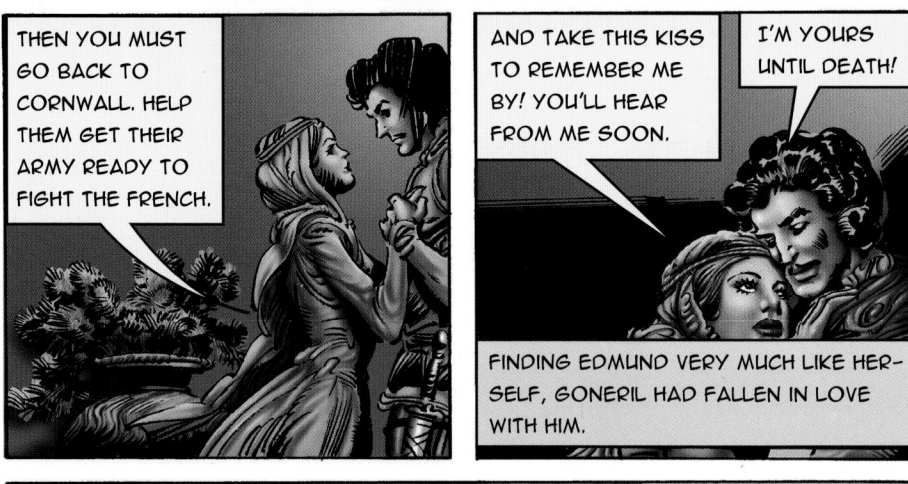

THEN YOU MUST GO BACK TO CORNWALL. HELP THEM GET THEIR ARMY READY TO FIGHT THE FRENCH.

AND TAKE THIS KISS TO REMEMBER ME BY! YOU'LL HEAR FROM ME SOON.

I'M YOURS UNTIL DEATH!

FINDING EDMUND VERY MUCH LIKE HERSELF, GONERIL HAD FALLEN IN LOVE WITH HIM.

AS EDMUND LEFT, THE DUKE OF ALBANY ENTERED THE ROOM. AND ALMOST AT THE SAME TIME, A MESSENGER ARRIVED.

CORNWALL HAS DIED FROM HIS WOUND!

THEN HE HAS BEEN PUNISHED FOR HIS CRUEL ACTIONS!

AND REGAN'S A WIDOW,* FREE TO MARRY EDMUND, WHOM I LOVE!

* a woman whose husband has died

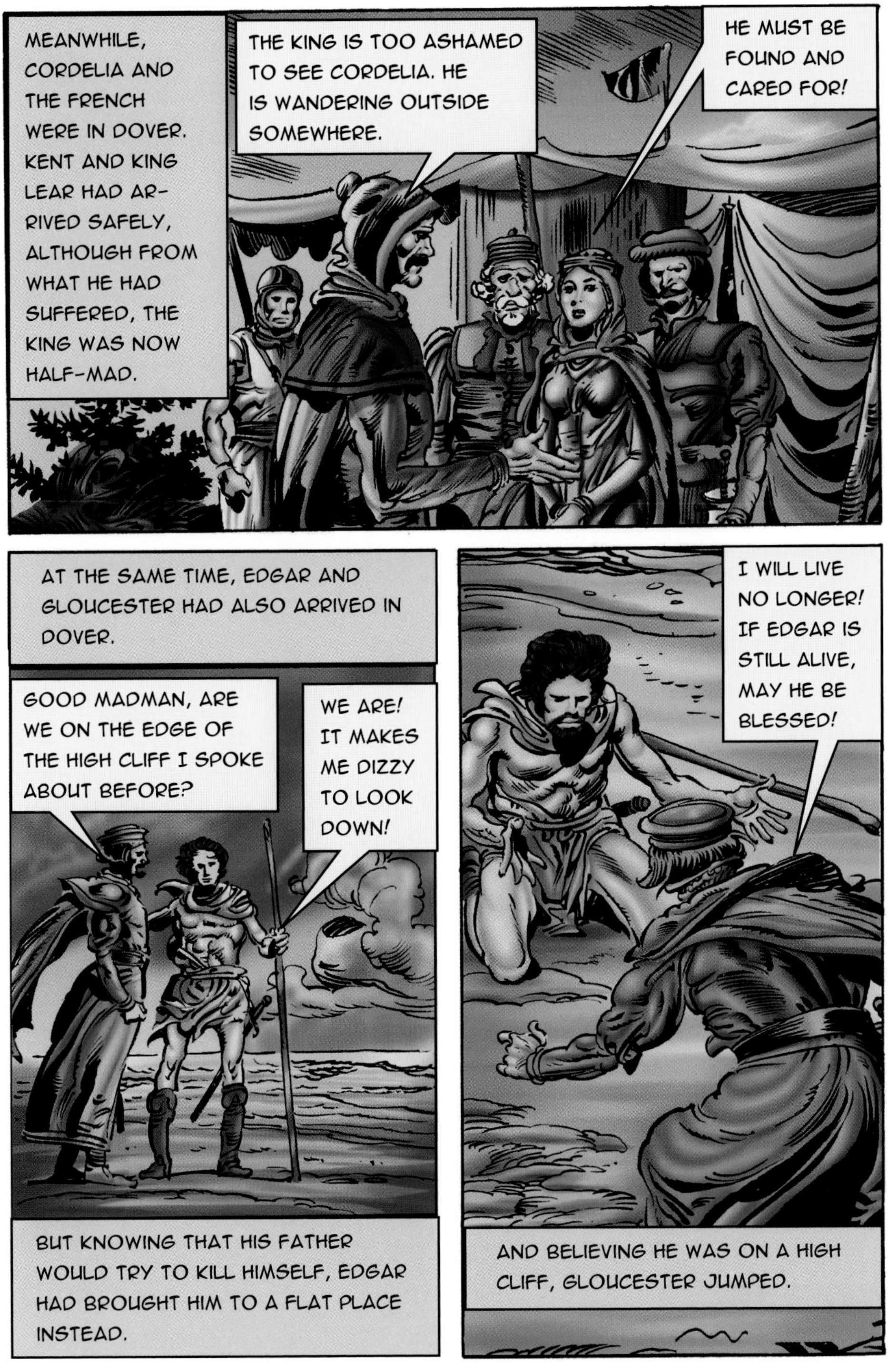
MEANWHILE, CORDELIA AND THE FRENCH WERE IN DOVER. KENT AND KING LEAR HAD ARRIVED SAFELY, ALTHOUGH FROM WHAT HE HAD SUFFERED, THE KING WAS NOW HALF-MAD.
THE KING IS TOO ASHAMED TO SEE CORDELIA. HE IS WANDERING OUTSIDE SOMEWHERE.
HE MUST BE FOUND AND CARED FOR!
AT THE SAME TIME, EDGAR AND GLOUCESTER HAD ALSO ARRIVED IN DOVER.
GOOD MADMAN, ARE WE ON THE EDGE OF THE HIGH CLIFF I SPOKE ABOUT BEFORE?
WE ARE! IT MAKES ME DIZZY TO LOOK DOWN!
BUT KNOWING THAT HIS FATHER WOULD TRY TO KILL HIMSELF, EDGAR HAD BROUGHT HIM TO A FLAT PLACE INSTEAD.
I WILL LIVE NO LONGER! IF EDGAR IS STILL ALIVE, MAY HE BE BLESSED!
AND BELIEVING HE WAS ON A HIGH CLIFF, GLOUCESTER JUMPED.

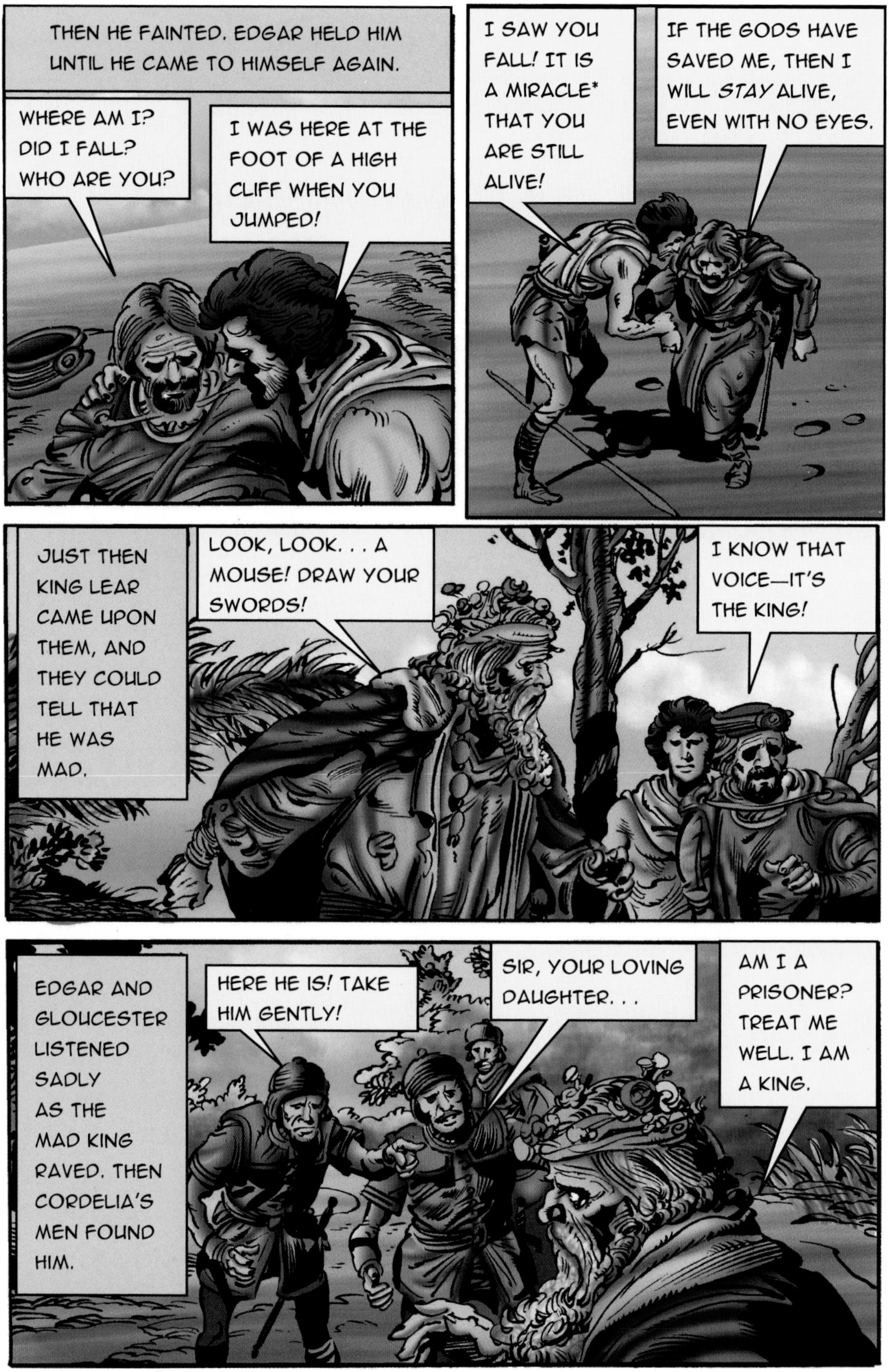
THEN HE FAINTED. EDGAR HELD HIM UNTIL HE CAME TO HIMSELF AGAIN.
WHERE AM I? DID I FALL? WHO ARE YOU?
I WAS HERE AT THE FOOT OF A HIGH CLIFF WHEN YOU JUMPED!
I SAW YOU FALL! IT IS A MIRACLE* THAT YOU ARE STILL ALIVE!
IF THE GODS HAVE SAVED ME, THEN I WILL *STAY* ALIVE, EVEN WITH NO EYES.
JUST THEN KING LEAR CAME UPON THEM, AND THEY COULD TELL THAT HE WAS MAD.
LOOK, LOOK. . . A MOUSE! DRAW YOUR SWORDS!
I KNOW THAT VOICE—IT'S THE KING!
EDGAR AND GLOUCESTER LISTENED SADLY AS THE MAD KING RAVED. THEN CORDELIA'S MEN FOUND HIM.
HERE HE IS! TAKE HIM GENTLY!
SIR, YOUR LOVING DAUGHTER. . .
AM I A PRISONER? TREAT ME WELL. I AM A KING.

* a wonderful happening that can't be explained or understood

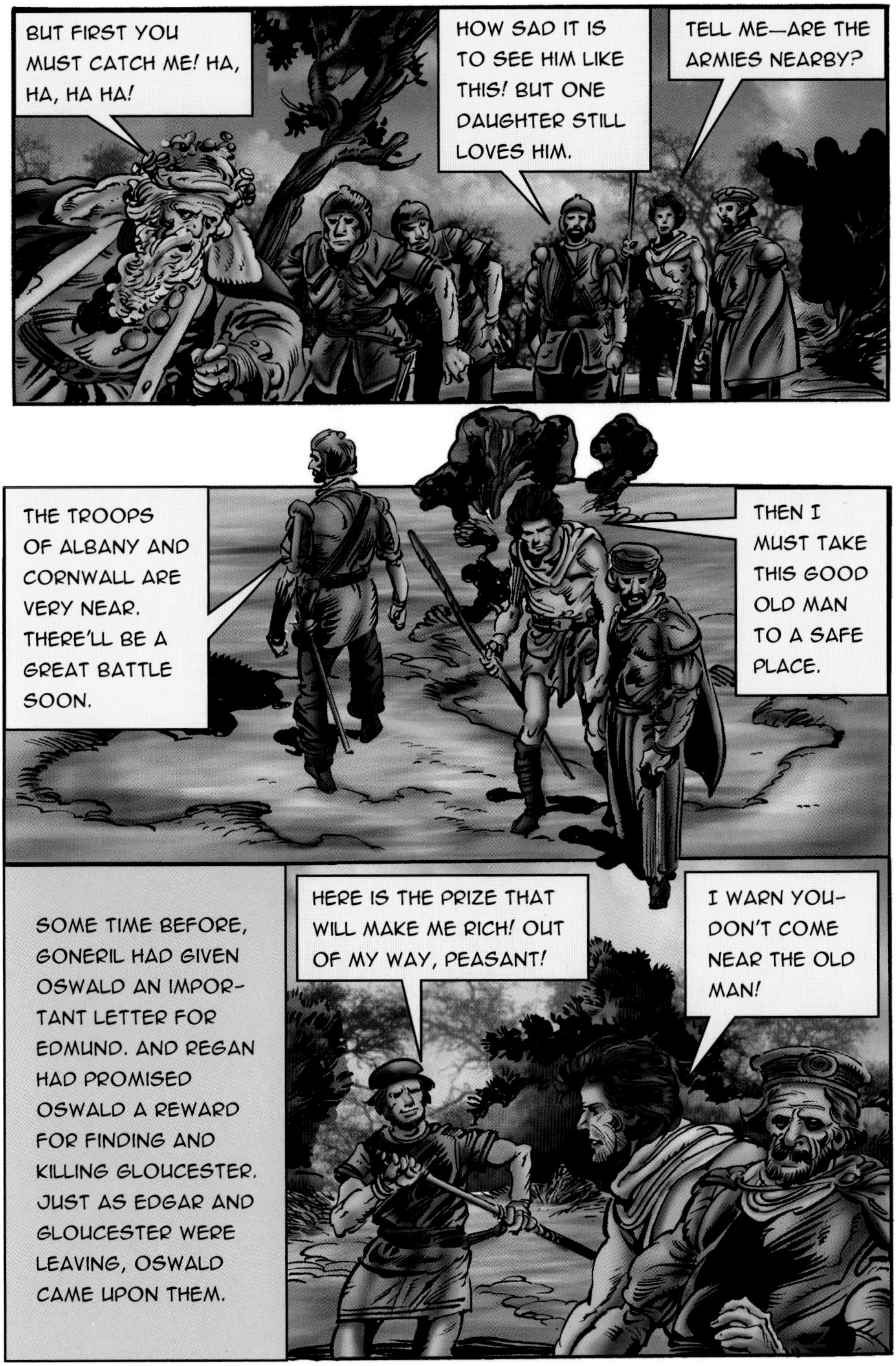
BUT FIRST YOU MUST CATCH ME! HA, HA, HA HA!
HOW SAD IT IS TO SEE HIM LIKE THIS! BUT ONE DAUGHTER STILL LOVES HIM.
TELL ME—ARE THE ARMIES NEARBY?
THE TROOPS OF ALBANY AND CORNWALL ARE VERY NEAR. THERE'LL BE A GREAT BATTLE SOON.
THEN I MUST TAKE THIS GOOD OLD MAN TO A SAFE PLACE.
SOME TIME BEFORE, GONERIL HAD GIVEN OSWALD AN IMPORTANT LETTER FOR EDMUND. AND REGAN HAD PROMISED OSWALD A REWARD FOR FINDING AND KILLING GLOUCESTER. JUST AS EDGAR AND GLOUCESTER WERE LEAVING, OSWALD CAME UPON THEM.
HERE IS THE PRIZE THAT WILL MAKE ME RICH! OUT OF MY WAY, PEASANT!
I WARN YOU— DON'T COME NEAR THE OLD MAN!

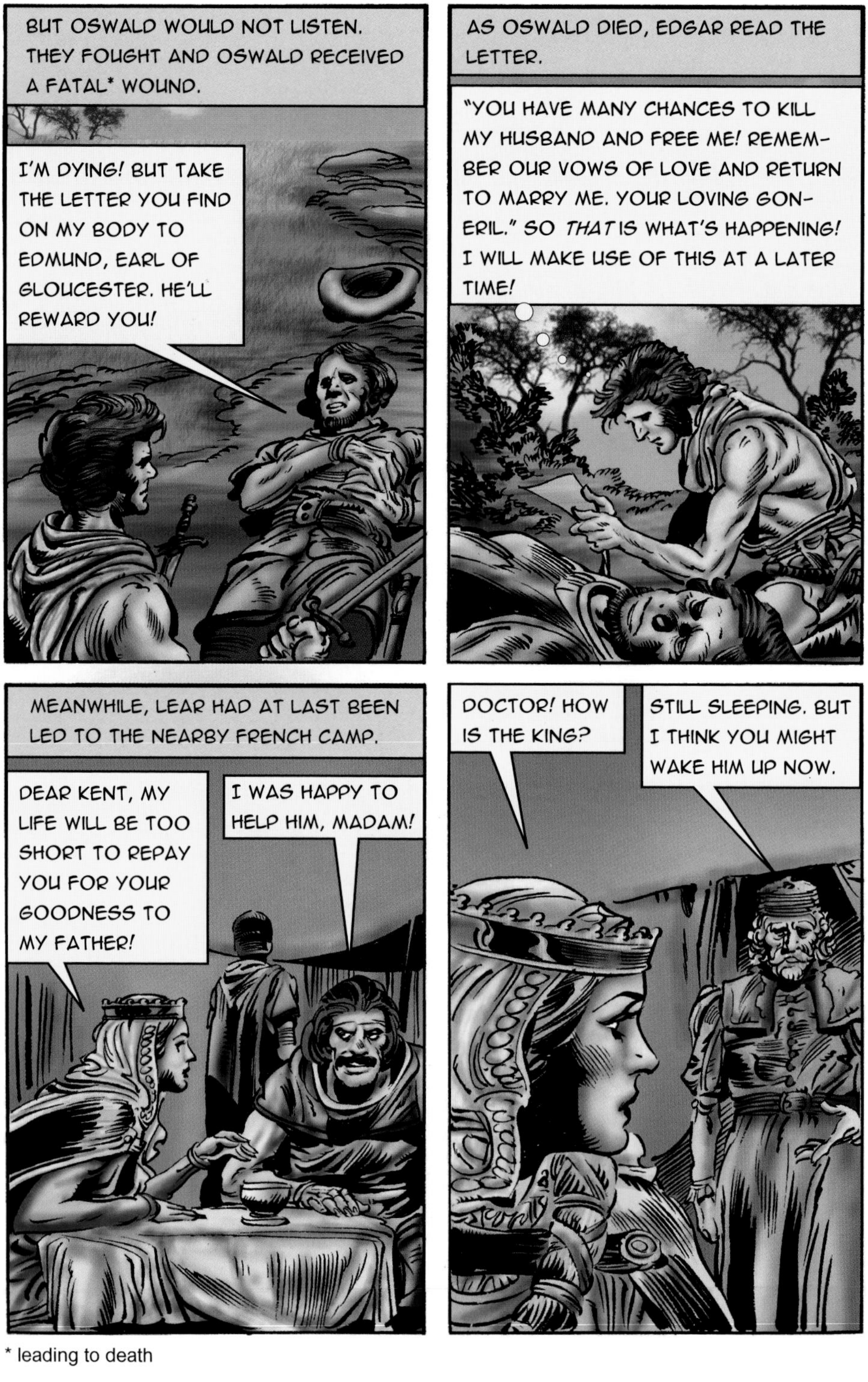
BUT OSWALD WOULD NOT LISTEN. THEY FOUGHT AND OSWALD RECEIVED A FATAL* WOUND.
I'M DYING! BUT TAKE THE LETTER YOU FIND ON MY BODY TO EDMUND, EARL OF GLOUCESTER. HE'LL REWARD YOU!
AS OSWALD DIED, EDGAR READ THE LETTER.
"YOU HAVE MANY CHANCES TO KILL MY HUSBAND AND FREE ME! REMEMBER OUR VOWS OF LOVE AND RETURN TO MARRY ME. YOUR LOVING GONERIL." SO *THAT* IS WHAT'S HAPPENING! I WILL MAKE USE OF THIS AT A LATER TIME!
MEANWHILE, LEAR HAD AT LAST BEEN LED TO THE NEARBY FRENCH CAMP.
DEAR KENT, MY LIFE WILL BE TOO SHORT TO REPAY YOU FOR YOUR GOODNESS TO MY FATHER!
I WAS HAPPY TO HELP HIM, MADAM!
DOCTOR! HOW IS THE KING?
STILL SLEEPING. BUT I THINK YOU MIGHT WAKE HIM UP NOW.

* leading to death

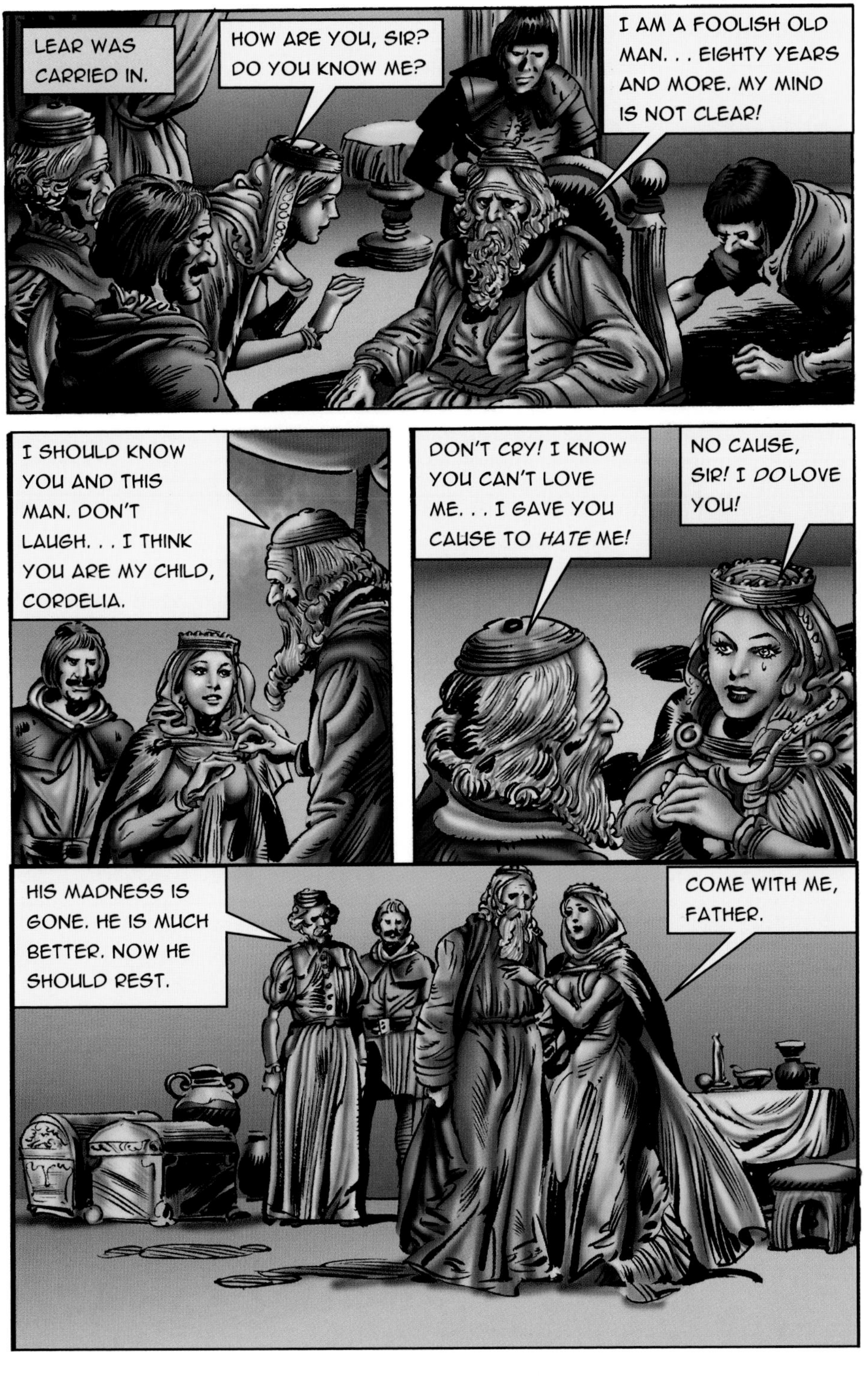
LEAR WAS CARRIED IN.
HOW ARE YOU, SIR? DO YOU KNOW ME?
I AM A FOOLISH OLD MAN. . . EIGHTY YEARS AND MORE. MY MIND IS NOT CLEAR!
I SHOULD KNOW YOU AND THIS MAN. DON'T LAUGH. . . I THINK YOU ARE MY CHILD, CORDELIA.
DON'T CRY! I KNOW YOU CAN'T LOVE ME. . . I GAVE YOU CAUSE TO *HATE* ME!
NO CAUSE, SIR! I *DO* LOVE YOU!
HIS MADNESS IS GONE. HE IS MUCH BETTER. NOW HE SHOULD REST.
COME WITH ME, FATHER.

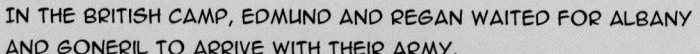

IN THE BRITISH CAMP, EDMUND AND REGAN WAITED FOR ALBANY AND GONERIL TO ARRIVE WITH THEIR ARMY.

I DON'T TRUST ALBANY! AND MY SISTER. . . ARE YOU IN LOVE WITH HER?

MY FEELINGS FOR YOUR SISTER ARE MOST HONORABLE!*

CORNWALL'S DEATH HAD MADE REGAN A WIDOW. SHE WAS JEALOUS** OF GONERIL BECAUSE SHE WAS NOW IN LOVE WITH EDMUND TOO.

SOON ALBANY AND GONERIL ARRIVED.

I WILL NOT FIGHT CORDELIA AND OUR KING—ONLY AGAINST THE FRENCH ARMIES WHO HAVE ENTERED OUR LAND.

WELL SPOKEN, SIR!

THERE'S REGAN. I'D RATHER LOSE THE BATTLE THAN LOSE EDMUND TO HER!

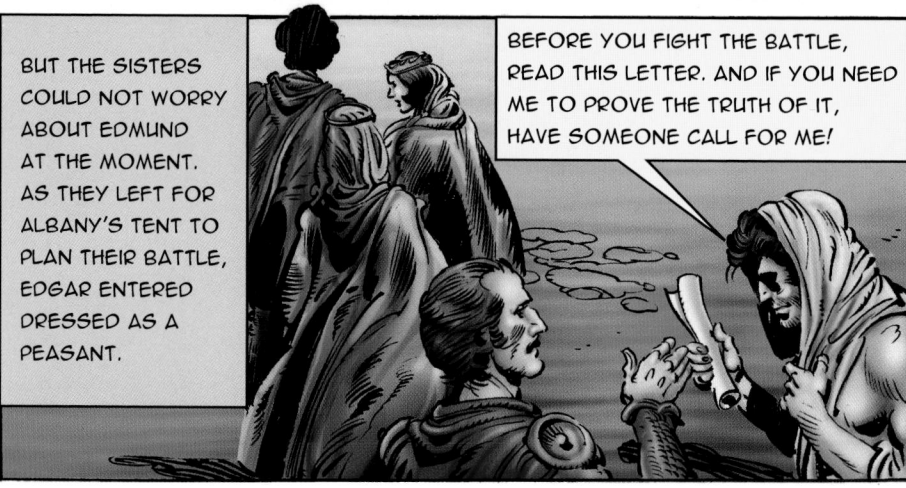

BUT THE SISTERS COULD NOT WORRY ABOUT EDMUND AT THE MOMENT. AS THEY LEFT FOR ALBANY'S TENT TO PLAN THEIR BATTLE, EDGAR ENTERED DRESSED AS A PEASANT.

BEFORE YOU FIGHT THE BATTLE, READ THIS LETTER. AND IF YOU NEED ME TO PROVE THE TRUTH OF IT, HAVE SOMEONE CALL FOR ME!

* correct, the way something is supposed to be

** wanting what someone else has

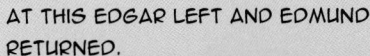

AT THIS EDGAR LEFT AND EDMUND RETURNED.

THE ENEMY'S HERE! GET READY.

WE ARE READY!

BOTH SISTERS LOVE ME AND ARE JEALOUS. REGAN IS ALREADY A WIDOW, BUT ALBANY MAY DIE IN BATTLE! WHICH ONE SHALL I CHOOSE?

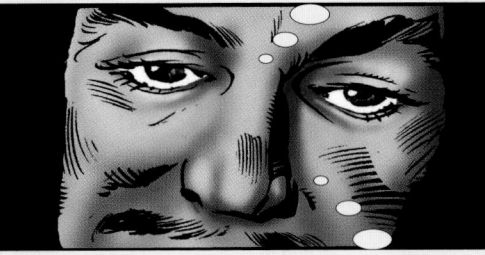

WELL IN ANY CASE, LEAR AND CORDE-LIA MUST DIE, EVEN THOUGH ALBANY WILL PROTECT THEM.

SOON THE ARMIES MET IN BATTLE. IN A SHORT TIME EVERYTHING WAS OVER, AND EDGAR RUSHED BACK TO GLOUCESTER.

COME QUICK. . . I'LL LEAD YOU TO SAFETY! THE FRENCH ARE BEATEN! CORDELIA AND LEAR ARE CAPTURED!

IN THE BRITISH CAMP, EDMUND WAS IN CHARGE.

TAKE THEM AWAY TO PRISON!

COME! WE TWO WILL LIVE LIKE BIRDS IN A CAGE TOGETHER!

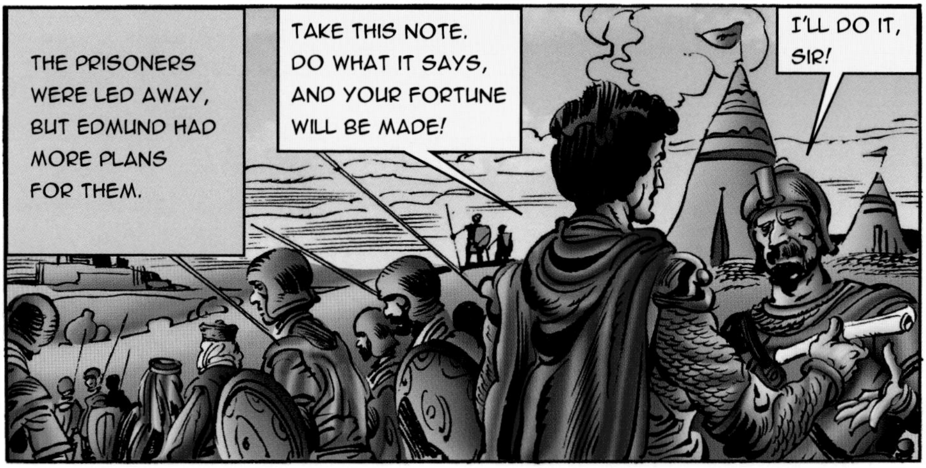
THE PRISONERS WERE LED AWAY, BUT EDMUND HAD MORE PLANS FOR THEM.
TAKE THIS NOTE. DO WHAT IT SAYS, AND YOUR FORTUNE WILL BE MADE!
I'LL DO IT, SIR!

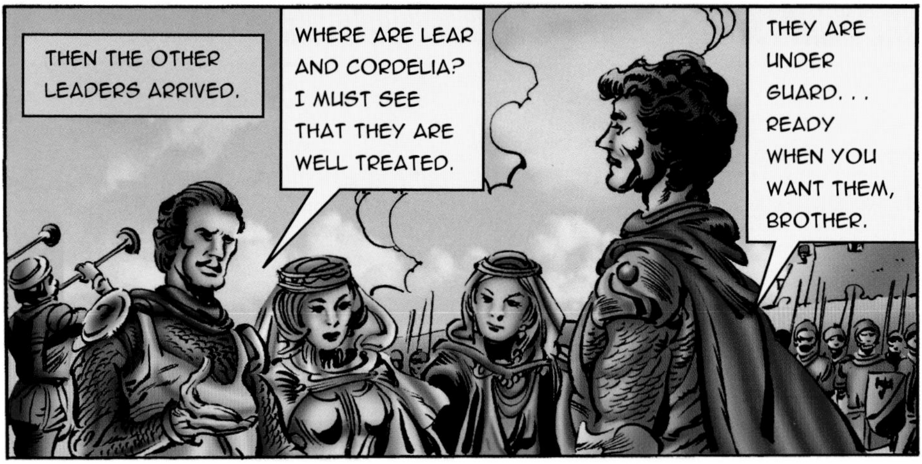
THEN THE OTHER LEADERS ARRIVED.
WHERE ARE LEAR AND CORDELIA? I MUST SEE THAT THEY ARE WELL TREATED.
THEY ARE UNDER GUARD. . . READY WHEN YOU WANT THEM, BROTHER.

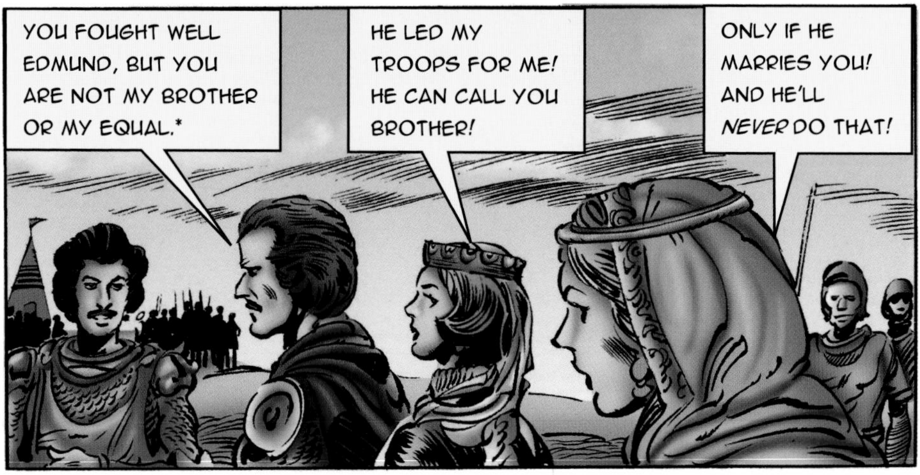
YOU FOUGHT WELL EDMUND, BUT YOU ARE NOT MY BROTHER OR MY EQUAL.*
HE LED MY TROOPS FOR ME! HE CAN CALL YOU BROTHER!
ONLY IF HE MARRIES YOU! AND HE'LL *NEVER* DO THAT!

* someone of the same class

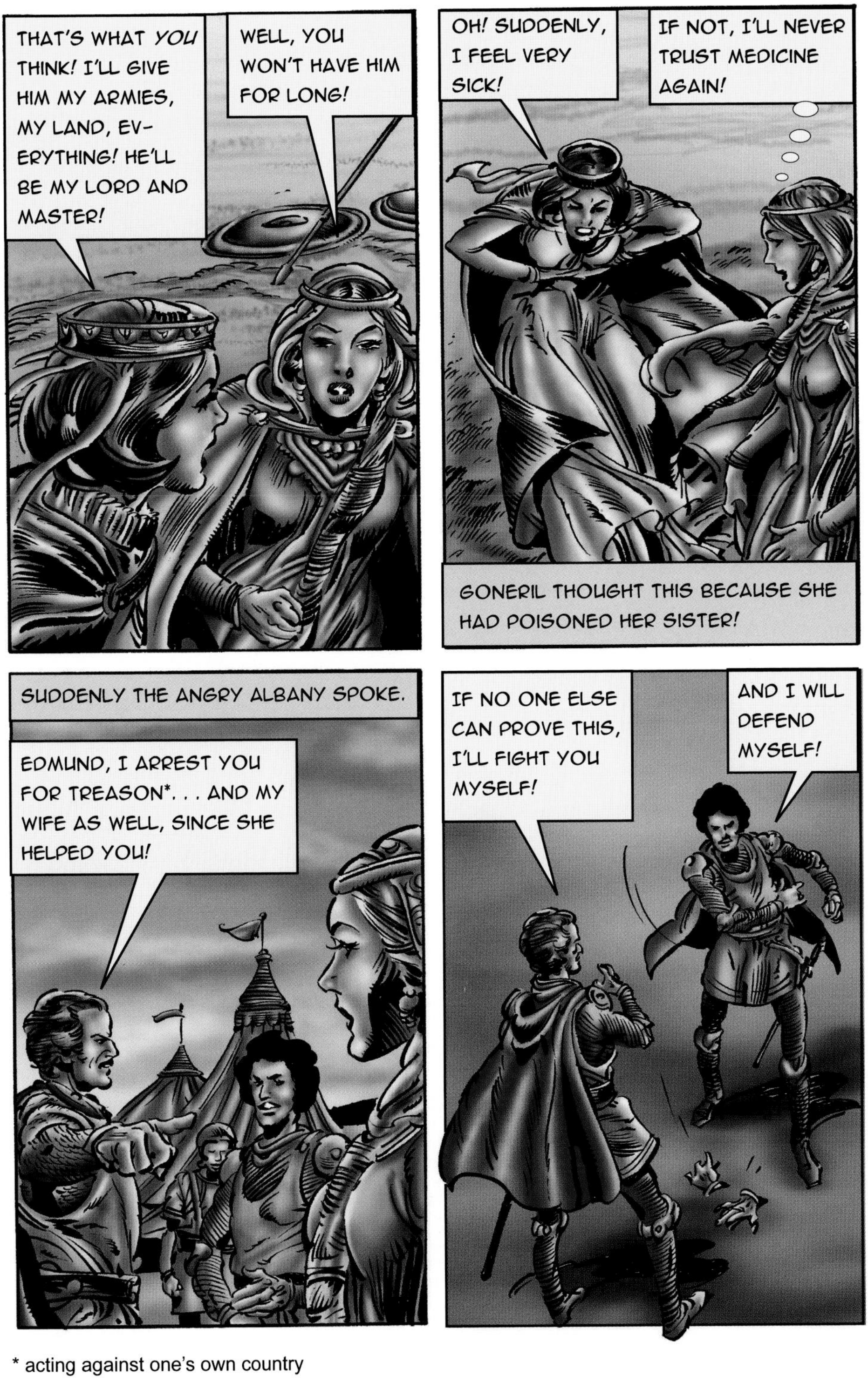
THAT'S WHAT *YOU* THINK! I'LL GIVE HIM MY ARMIES, MY LAND, EV- ERYTHING! HE'LL BE MY LORD AND MASTER!
WELL, YOU WON'T HAVE HIM FOR LONG!
OH! SUDDENLY, I FEEL VERY SICK!
IF NOT, I'LL NEVER TRUST MEDICINE AGAIN!
GONERIL THOUGHT THIS BECAUSE SHE HAD POISONED HER SISTER!
SUDDENLY THE ANGRY ALBANY SPOKE.
EDMUND, I ARREST YOU FOR TREASON*. . . AND MY WIFE AS WELL, SINCE SHE HELPED YOU!
IF NO ONE ELSE CAN PROVE THIS, I'LL FIGHT YOU MYSELF!
AND I WILL DEFEND MYSELF!

* acting against one's own country

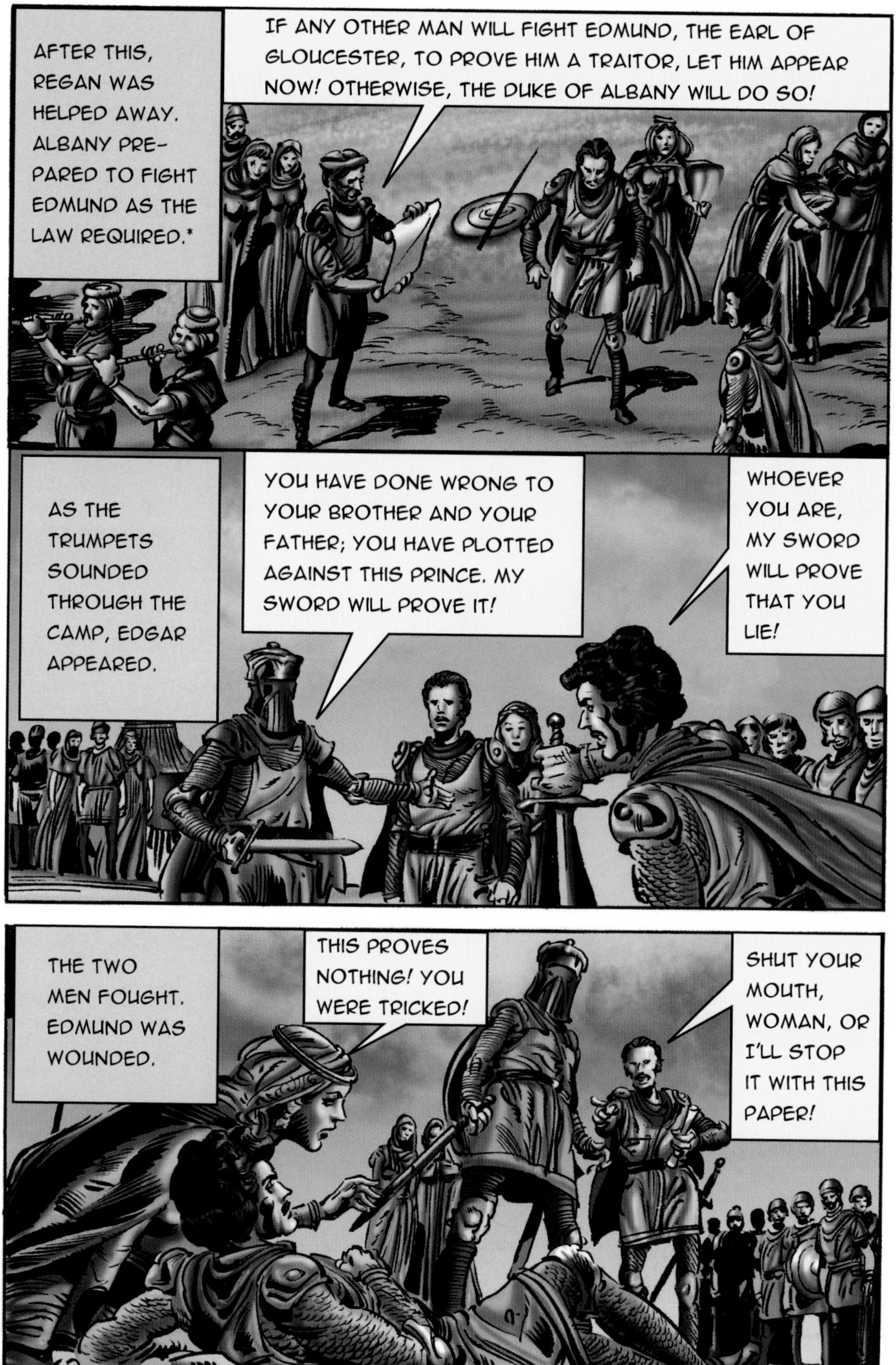
AFTER THIS, REGAN WAS HELPED AWAY. ALBANY PRE-PARED TO FIGHT EDMUND AS THE LAW REQUIRED.*
IF ANY OTHER MAN WILL FIGHT EDMUND, THE EARL OF GLOUCESTER, TO PROVE HIM A TRAITOR, LET HIM APPEAR NOW! OTHERWISE, THE DUKE OF ALBANY WILL DO SO!
AS THE TRUMPETS SOUNDED THROUGH THE CAMP, EDGAR APPEARED.
YOU HAVE DONE WRONG TO YOUR BROTHER AND YOUR FATHER; YOU HAVE PLOTTED AGAINST THIS PRINCE. MY SWORD WILL PROVE IT!
WHOEVER YOU ARE, MY SWORD WILL PROVE THAT YOU LIE!
THE TWO MEN FOUGHT. EDMUND WAS WOUNDED.
THIS PROVES NOTHING! YOU WERE TRICKED!
SHUT YOUR MOUTH, WOMAN, OR I'LL STOP IT WITH THIS PAPER!

* made necessary

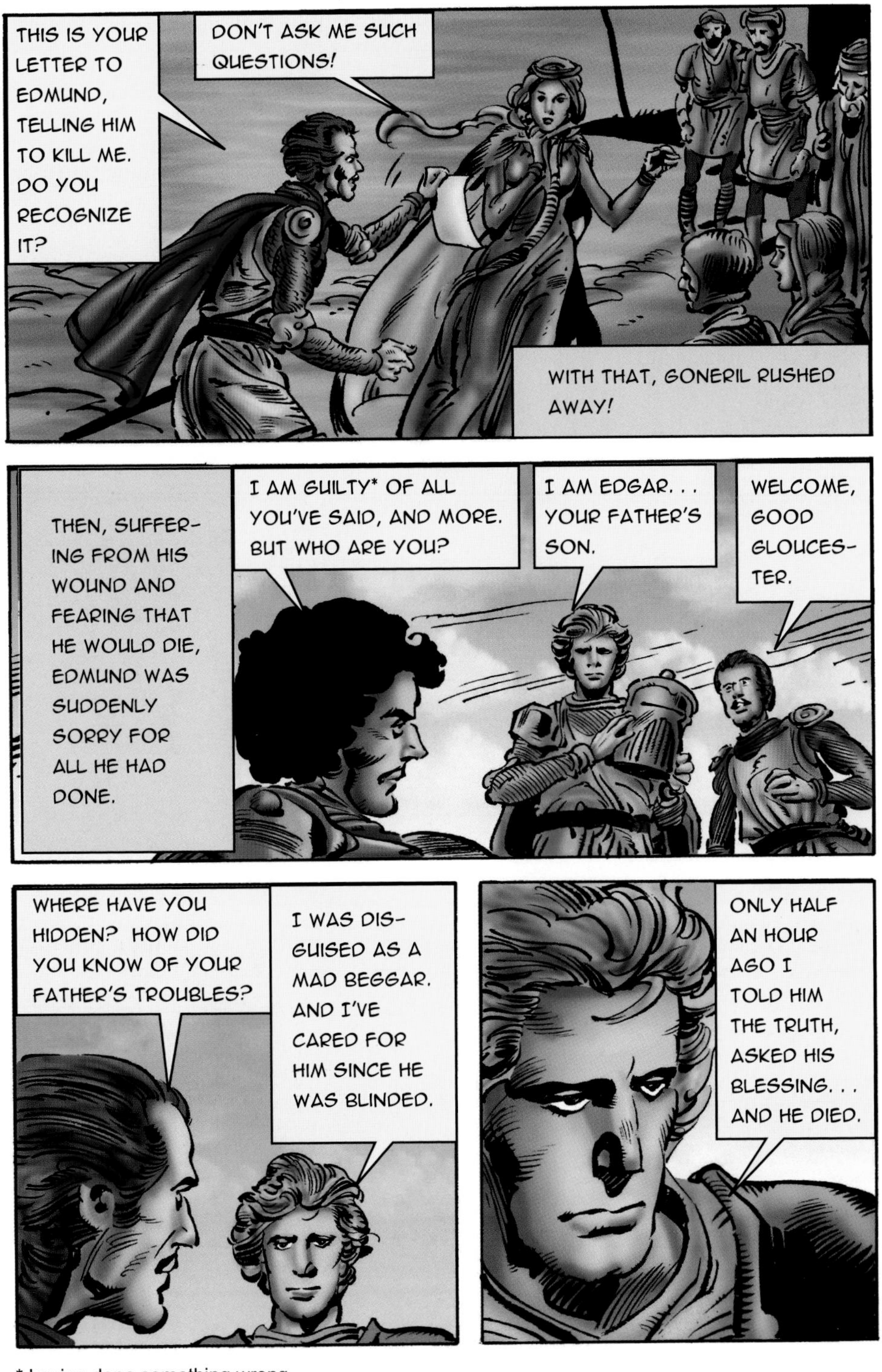
THIS IS YOUR LETTER TO EDMUND, TELLING HIM TO KILL ME. DO YOU RECOGNIZE IT?
DON'T ASK ME SUCH QUESTIONS!
WITH THAT, GONERIL RUSHED AWAY!
THEN, SUFFERING FROM HIS WOUND AND FEARING THAT HE WOULD DIE, EDMUND WAS SUDDENLY SORRY FOR ALL HE HAD DONE.
I AM GUILTY* OF ALL YOU'VE SAID, AND MORE. BUT WHO ARE YOU?
I AM EDGAR. . . YOUR FATHER'S SON.
WELCOME, GOOD GLOUCESTER.
WHERE HAVE YOU HIDDEN? HOW DID YOU KNOW OF YOUR FATHER'S TROUBLES?
I WAS DISGUISED AS A MAD BEGGAR. AND I'VE CARED FOR HIM SINCE HE WAS BLINDED.
ONLY HALF AN HOUR AGO I TOLD HIM THE TRUTH, ASKED HIS BLESSING. . . AND HE DIED.

* having done something wrong

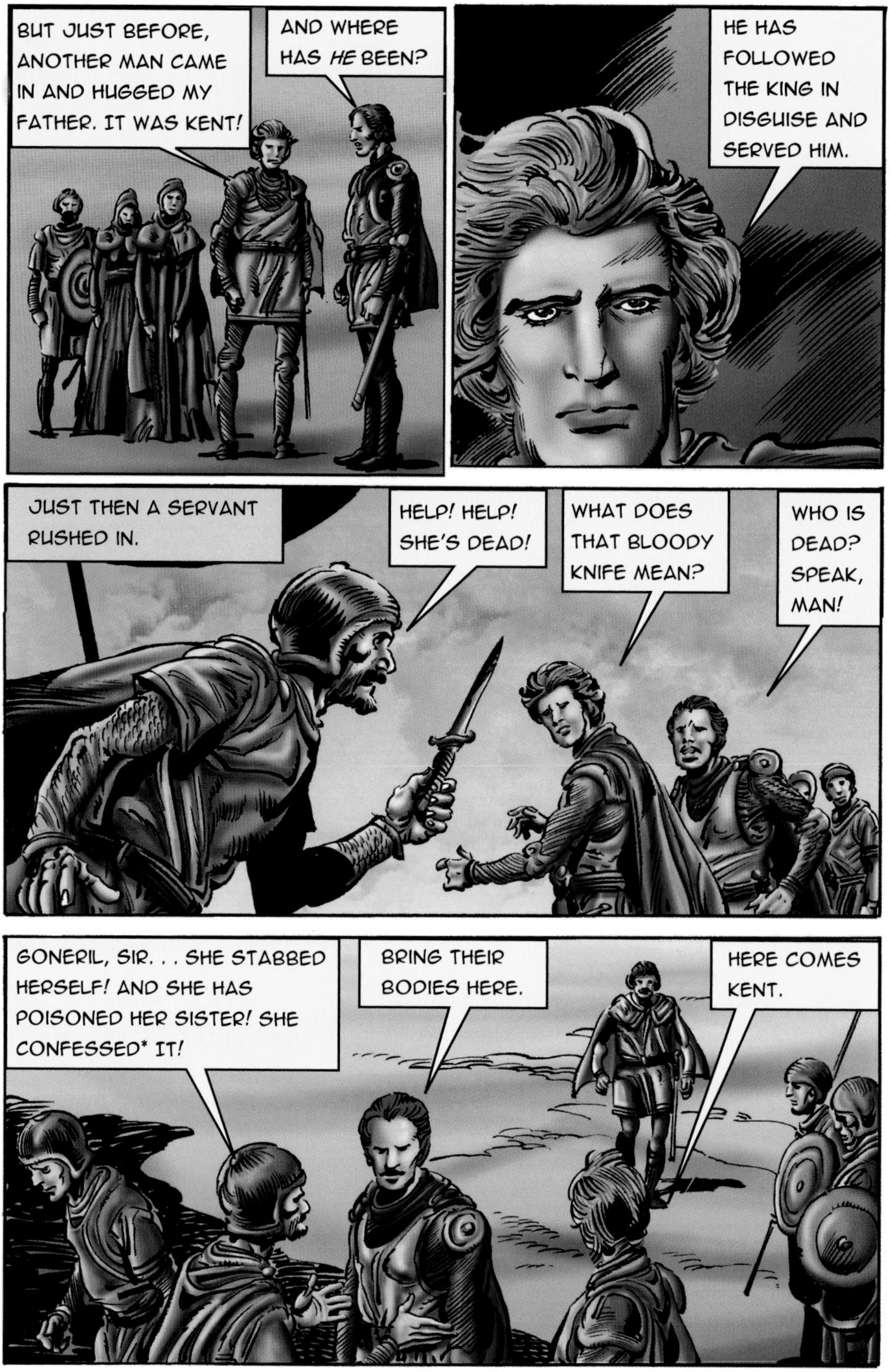
BUT JUST BEFORE, ANOTHER MAN CAME IN AND HUGGED MY FATHER. IT WAS KENT!
AND WHERE HAS *HE* BEEN?
HE HAS FOLLOWED THE KING IN DISGUISE AND SERVED HIM.
JUST THEN A SERVANT RUSHED IN.
HELP! HELP! SHE'S DEAD!
WHAT DOES THAT BLOODY KNIFE MEAN?
WHO IS DEAD? SPEAK, MAN!
GONERIL, SIR. . . SHE STABBED HERSELF! AND SHE HAS POISONED HER SISTER! SHE CONFESSED* IT!
BRING THEIR BODIES HERE.
HERE COMES KENT.

* admitted

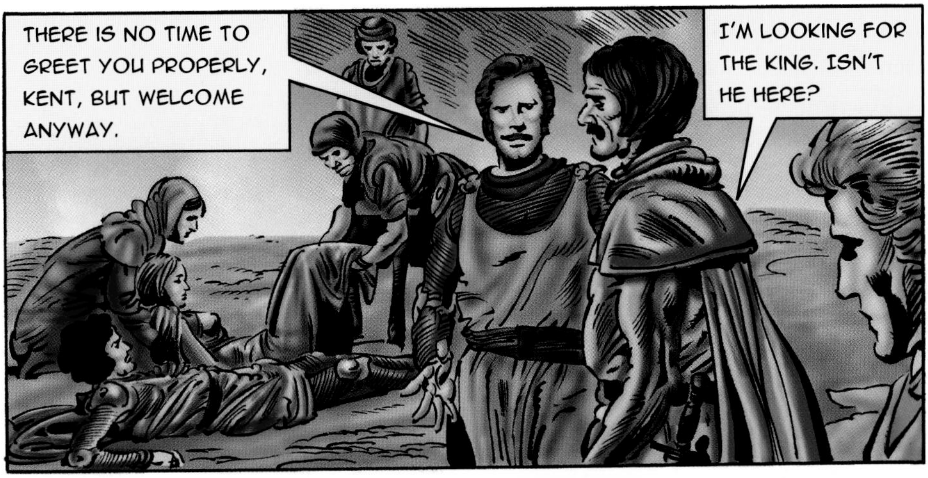
THERE IS NO TIME TO GREET YOU PROPERLY, KENT, BUT WELCOME ANYWAY.
I'M LOOKING FOR THE KING. ISN'T HE HERE?

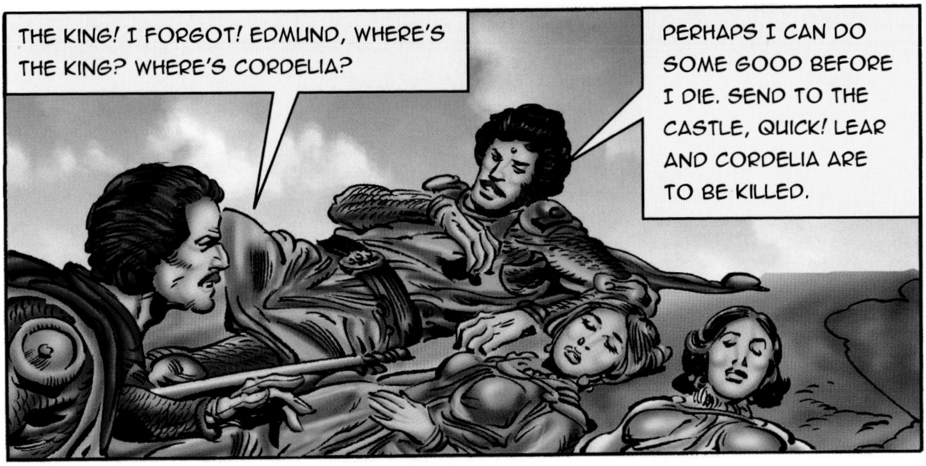
THE KING! I FORGOT! EDMUND, WHERE'S THE KING? WHERE'S CORDELIA?
PERHAPS I CAN DO SOME GOOD BEFORE I DIE. SEND TO THE CASTLE, QUICK! LEAR AND CORDELIA ARE TO BE KILLED.

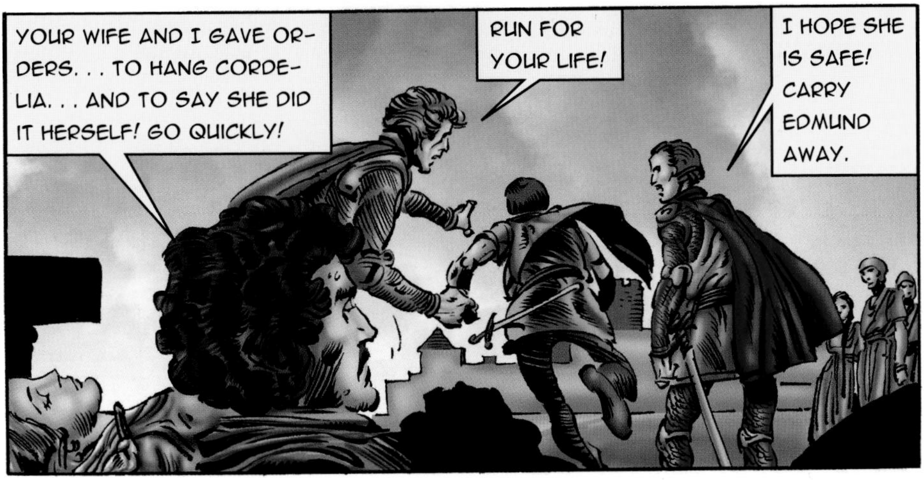
YOUR WIFE AND I GAVE OR-DERS. . . TO HANG CORDE-LIA. . . AND TO SAY SHE DID IT HERSELF! GO QUICKLY!
RUN FOR YOUR LIFE!
I HOPE SHE IS SAFE! CARRY EDMUND AWAY.

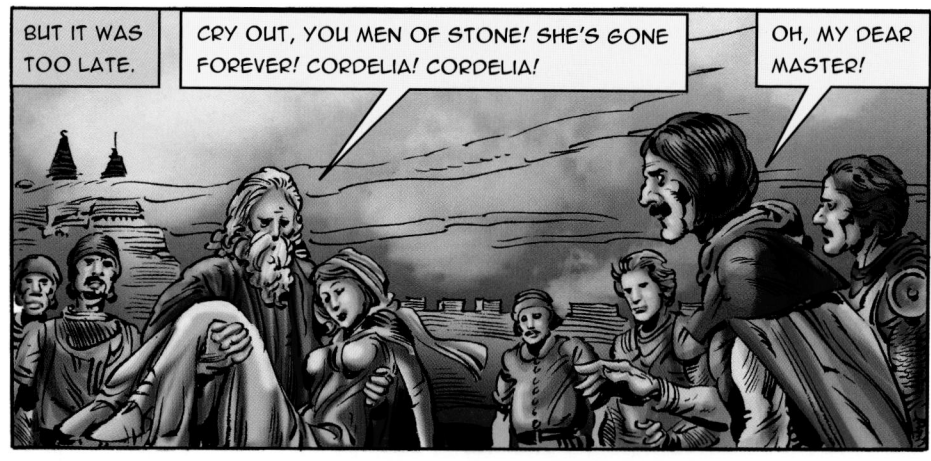

BUT IT WAS TOO LATE.

CRY OUT, YOU MEN OF STONE! SHE'S GONE FOREVER! CORDELIA! CORDELIA!

OH, MY DEAR MASTER!

CORDELIA, STAY! WHAT ARE YOU SAYING? I KILLED THE MAN THAT WAS HANGING YOU.

IT'S TRUE, GENTLEMEN, HE DID.

MY POOR DEAR IS DEAD. I'LL NEVER SEE HER AGAIN. . . NEVER, NEVER, NEVER, NEVER, NEVER!

HE FAINTED! HELP HIM!

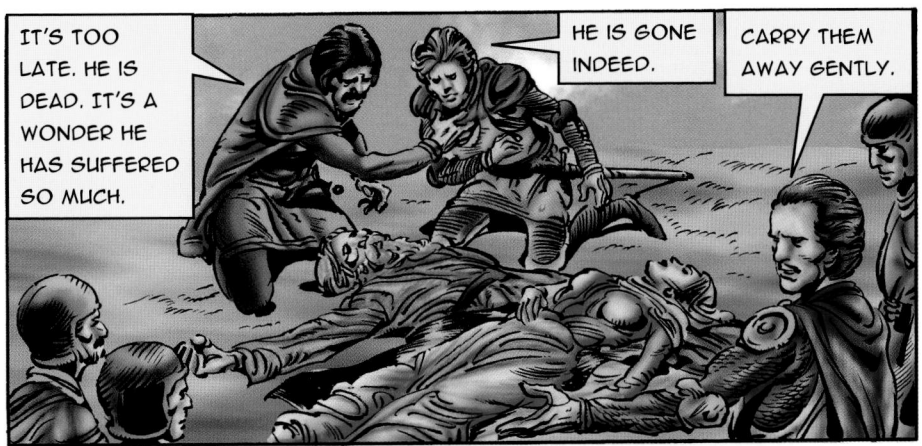

IT'S TOO LATE. HE IS DEAD. IT'S A WONDER HE HAS SUFFERED SO MUCH.

HE IS GONE INDEED.

CARRY THEM AWAY GENTLY.

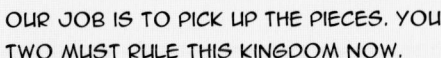

OUR JOB IS TO PICK UP THE PIECES. YOU TWO MUST RULE THIS KINGDOM NOW.

NO, SIR. EDGAR MUST RULE ALONE.

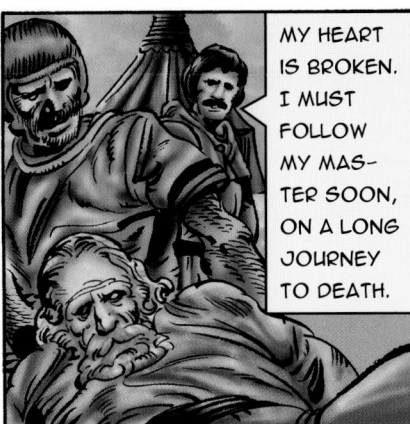

MY HEART IS BROKEN. I MUST FOLLOW MY MASTER SOON, ON A LONG JOURNEY TO DEATH.

LEAR, CORDELIA, GLOUCESTER, EDMUND, REGAN, GONERIL—ALL WERE DEAD. FOR THOSE WHO WERE LEFT, ONLY A SAD FUNERAL MARCH REMAINED.

YES, I WILL RULE THIS LAND. AND NOTHING LIKE THIS SHALL EVER HAPPEN AGAIN!

THE END